BIGFOOT: THE DARK SIDE

BIGFOOT: THE
DARK SIDE

RUSTY WILSON

ISBN: 978-1-948859-03-5

For all who like adventure and mystery
And for Aleksandra

CONTENTS

FOREWORD

Ready for stories about the scarier side of Bigfoot by the World's Greatest Bigfoot Story Teller?

Fly-fishing guide Rusty Wilson spent years collecting these tales from his clients around the campfire, stories guaranteed to make sure you won't want to go out after dark.

Be sure to go to a friend's house to read them, because you won't want to be alone, and whatever you do, don't walk home by yourself!

Come read about a most unusual resort house in Washington's Palouse country—then read about the strange Yellowstone Fog and the secrets it holds—come along to mysterious Alaska where an archaeologist makes a find he wishes he hadn't—find out if a human can outwit a bloodthirsty Bigfoot by climbing high in a tree—visit a unique house set in the Utah desert—then climb high on Canada's highest peak where something malevolent awaits you.

Another great book from Rusty Wilson, Bigfoot expert and storyteller—tales for both the Bigfoot believer and those who just enjoy a good story.

INTRODUCTION

Greetings, fellow adventures, to this collection of Bigfoot campfire stories featuring the dark side of the Big Guy, a side I hope to never meet, and a side that I also hope you never meet. To me, Bigfoot is frightening enough without also knowing he's out to get you.

Like most of my stories, these were collected around campfires, told by my fly-fishing clients, though some were told to me in person. Fortunately, none of these events happened to me, and hearing about them has made me much warier of being alone out in the wilds.

Much controversy exists in the Bigfoot world as to whether or not these elusive creatures are benign or dangerous, but I personally think they're much like we are in that some are friendlier than others. I'm sure each has their own personality, and probably even the nicest ones have bad hair days. And given how we humans are encroaching more and more on their habitat, I think I might get a little grumpy now and then too, if it were me.

In any case, I hope you enjoy these tales from the dark side, and I also hope they remind you to keep your eyes open when you're out in the wilds, especially after dark.

So, sit back with a cup of hot chocolate in a big comfy chair or by a campfire and enjoy. Just be sure to lock the door, or if you don't have a door, keep a can of bear spray handy. —Rusty

1

LOOSE IN THE PALOUSE

My wife Sarah and I stopped in a park in Spokane, Washington, for a break on our way up to a friend's wedding, when I noticed a nearby SUV with the kind of heavy plastic tubes on top that fishermen use to carry their rods.

I said hello to the elderly gent standing next to the vehicle, asking him if he fished. Well, he did, and one thing led to another, and we were soon engaged in conversation. This in turn led to the following story, after I'd told him I collect Bigfoot tales.

His name was George, and he told this with such conviction that I truly believe it happened. I invited him to come visit us in Colorado, and I sincerely hope he does. —Rusty

I'm retired, so I have lots of free time, and that free time is exactly what led me into the most disturbing thing I've ever had happen in all my 74 years. And I think that part of what made it so scary was that it was so unexpected. I wasn't out in the wilds, but in one of the most tamed and cultivated landscapes you can find.

I was looking for something to photograph, or I would've never ended up in the Palouse country of southeast Washington, a place so pretty and benign that I would never have guessed I would someday have nightmares about it.

But let me back up a little. I retired fairly young at 58, and my wife and I started doing a lot of traveling, which led her to decide she didn't want to be with me. She was used to me working and didn't like my companionship 24/7, which I can understand.

What I can't understand is why she felt it necessary to get a divorce just when our life together could've been really good. Up to then, all we'd both done is work, and now that we were free to do whatever we wanted, she left.

What I found out later was that she left me for another guy, and it had nothing to do with spending time together. She was simply in love with someone else.

Either way, it hurt, and I needed something to distract me from all that, so I joined a local photography club.

Even though I was retired, I wasn't an old geezer yet, though most of the club members were older guys. At first, I felt really out of place, but I soon made some good friends and really got into the monthly club outings. In addition, there were meetings where we would analyze each other's photos, and we even had a couple of photography shows each year that were juried.

When I started winning a few ribbons, I found I was totally hooked. Through time, I spent a fortune on equipment until I was in up to my eyeballs with thousands of dollars in equipment. I could afford it, as I'd been an executive with a pharmaceutical company and had made good money.

As time went by, I myself became one of the old geezers in the club, and I racked up a lot of travel all over the world, going on various photography tours to places like Iceland to shoot the Aurora, and Manitoba to film polar bears.

But I finally realized that one of the best photography places in the world was right in my backyard and less than an hour away—the Palouse. And the Palouse turned out to be home to one of the wildest things one could ever imagine.

The Palouse is one of the most serene and pastoral regions in the world, rolling hills covered with wheat fields, though they also grow other dry-land crops such as canola, barley, and peas. The hills were formed over tens of thousands of years from wind-blown silt and look like giant cultivated sand dunes.

In the spring, the fields are numerous pastel shades of green when the wheat and barley are new, and in the summer and fall the fields turn shades of brown and gold when the crops mature and are ready for harvest. With all the different colors and contoured hills, the area is truly heaven for photographers. This beautiful place was only an hour or so from my house.

As you know, photographers value what we call the golden hours (sunrise and sunset), as well as the blue hour, that time after sunset when everything turns a deep blue. I particularly liked the blue hour, but it was hard for me at my age to drive in the dark, which I would have to do if I wanted to be in the Palouse at that time of day.

So, I continually looked on the internet and in newspaper ads to see if there were any places in the Palouse where I could spend the night. Most of the larger towns in the area have motels, but I wanted to be as close to the rural areas as possible, and these small farm towns typically had no such accommodations, as the Palouse isn't really tourist country.

But one day, I got a call from my daughter, Marti, who lives over in Sandpoint, not too far from Spokane. Marti knew I was looking for a place in the Palouse, and she sounded excited.

"Dad," she said. "I just saw an ad for a new resort rental near Palouse. It says it's in the heart of the Palouse country, in a little town called Colfax. Do you know where that is?"

"Yes," I answered. "It's not far from Steptoe Butte. It would be perfect. The actual town of Palouse is nearby, also."

Marti emailed me a link to the property, which was being advertised on a well-known overnight-rental site.

The ad described a place on the main street of the town with big windows where one could sit and watch the non-existent traffic go by.

The photos showed what looked to be a combination of a New York loft and brew pub, with high ceilings and brick walls. It was part of a remodeled historic building, with a butcher shop on one side of the big building and the apartment on the other.

"This is our personal home, so you're not going to get a perfect fancy schmancy place, but it's comfortable and clean and perfectly located for photographers," the description read. "We've included a Washington State Discovery pass to Steptoe Butte, which is only a few miles away. The owner is a photographer and has included a folder of 'secret' nearby places where you can take photos of old bridges, old barns, and endless fields, all of which will make your trip to the Palouse special. We own the butcher shop next door, but my husband is also an auctioneer, which takes us away quite frequently. If you check the calendar, you'll see the times when we're away and our home is available."

It seemed too good to be true! I had finally found a place in the heart of the Palouse, and to top things off, it belonged to a fellow photographer!

I called Marti back to thank her, and we talked a little about family stuff, but I soon hung up, as I was eager to get online and make a reservation for the place in Colfax.

It was open that very next week, which was great, as it was early summer, one of the prime times to visit the area, as the fields would be starting to green up. I made the reservation for the entire week, then set to gathering up my photography equipment and everything I would need, for I would leave the very next day.

I was very excited—a whole week in the Palouse during one of the best times to visit, and no driving very far in the dark!

I arrived at what I'll call the Butcher's House the next afternoon, punched in the code to the lock, and walked inside. It looked just like the photos, except it was much larger.

In the wall of the anteroom was a large heavy door that I guessed must lead into the butcher shop section of the building. It was locked, and a sign on it read, "Please do not enter."

I noted that this particular room had a strange musky odor to it, an odor that seemed to come from the vicinity of the door, so I decided it must be coming from the butcher shop.

In any case, the smell was somewhat unpleasant, and I was disappointed that the proprietor of the nightly rental hadn't at the very least done something to mask the odor, such as burning a scented candle or such.

I unloaded my stuff, and since it was now late afternoon, headed out to find a good place to take some sunset photos. I wanted to maximize every minute in the Palouse, even though I had a glorious week to do nothing but take pictures.

I ended up driving to the small town of Palouse itself, taking my time along the way and getting lots of photos. At one point, I pulled off the road and climbed up a small hill where I could see quite a ways, the landscape zigzagging with fields of green and brown and gold where the spring wheat was starting to mature and ripen.

What makes the Palouse so special is all the rolling hills, some so steep that you wonder how they could be cultivated. In fact, I read later that some of the hills in the Palouse are steep enough to cause tractors and combines to tip over.

A Palouse farmer had invented a control mechanism that led to the development of self-leveling combines, which makes it possible for the header to follow the slope of the hill, while the cab and body remain level. In any case, all the topsy-turvy fields of different colors make for some wonderful landscape photography.

By the time I got the 20 or so miles to the town of Palouse, I'd already taken a couple of hundred photos. I usually get about five or 10 keepers per hundred, so I was excited to see what they would look like when I got back to the Butcher's House.

I had dinner at a restaurant there in Palouse, and by then it was dark, so I drove the 17 miles back to the little town of Colfax, watching carefully for deer and wildlife. Even though the Palouse is 98 percent cultivated, there are still some critters that manage to make it their home.

Back at the Butcher's House, I realized I'd forgotten to leave a light on, and I fumbled my way inside until I found a light switch. The musty odor was still there, and it seemed a bit stronger in the ante-room where the mysterious door was. I didn't think much about it, being pretty sure the odor was coming from the butcher shop.

The Butcher's House had one small wing that went back into what was the owners' bedroom, a private bath, a laundry room, and a small TV room with a big comfy leather couch. The rest of the house was a large living room/kitchen combination that looked out to the street through big store-front windows.

I'd been told I was welcome to sleep in the master wing, but I decided I liked the second bedroom more, which was adjacent to the small anteroom and thereby close to the front door.

I think even that early in the game I was feeling a bit uneasy, wanting to be close to an escape route, as the back part of the house didn't have any way out except through an emergency window. But it could've just been my little bit of claustrophobia rearing its head, as I've never liked places that weren't open, well lit, and easy to get into and out of.

I was tired, and the house was remarkably quiet, so I slept well. The next day was spent driving around looking for good places to take sunset photos, as well as visiting an old cemetery and taking photos there. I'm not really much of a cemetery fan, but one of my camera-club assignments was to take photos in a cemetery, so I figured I would kill two birds with one stone.

I went back to the house in the early afternoon to take a break. I ended up taking a nap, which was totally unlike me, as the few times I've napped in the past I end up not being able to sleep at night, so I usually avoid them.

I was asleep for a couple of hours. I decided it was because of the stone quiet in the Butcher's House, which was really nice. Of course it wasn't just the house, as the small-town had very little going on.

I had a great evening and got some good sunset photos, then came home and had a TV dinner and went to bed, sleeping like a baby in spite of the nap.

The next day was pretty much a repeat of the first day, except I went to the little grocery store and got some decent food to eat, mostly some salad stuff and tea and juice. After a late dinner, I was about ready to go to bed, but I first decided to take a look at the photos I'd taken that day.

I usually download them on my computer, but I was too tired, so I turned off all the lights so I could see the LED screen on my camera better and started going through the photos. I was very happy with what I saw, thinking that I was getting some pretty darn good shots and feeling that it was about time, seeing how much money I'd spent on my photography hobby. These seemed to be some of the best pictures I'd taken to date.

As I sat there in the dark, I looked up just in time to see something across the street. The front of the Butcher's House was pretty much all fixed glass with a couple of small windows on each side which I had opened to let some of the cool night air inside. I don't know what kind of business it had once been, but maybe something like a furniture store with its big showcase windows. I had a good view of the street, at least where the street lights were shining down through the dark.

I knew I'd seen movement, but I figured it must just be an alley cat or something, and I went back to looking at my photos. When I was done, I turned my camera off and sat there in the dark, tired. I needed to get up and go to bed, but I was worn out from all the activity. I'm not a young man, and I usually do pretty good, but sometimes I get weary.

I felt like I could nod off right then and there, but suddenly, from nowhere, I was wide-awake and energized. I felt my scalp begin to tingle, something I've only felt one other time in my entire life, and that was when I was out hiking and looked up to see a mountain lion not more than 30 feet ahead of me. It bolted when it realized I was there, but I'll never forget that feeling.

I was instantly on guard, but I couldn't figure out why, until I again saw movement across the street. A small alleyway opened opposite the front of the house, and I saw something very large and black standing there. I didn't know what it was, but it gave me the creeps.

Even though I was panicked, I very slowly got up and quietly closed the two side windows, then stepped back into the shadows so the light coming in from the street lamp in front of the house wouldn't shine on me. I then slipped into the anteroom and checked the door to make sure it was locked, then stood back a little where I could see out the front and yet not be seen.

The figure was gone, and now I could hear what sounded like trash cans being rattled around. It had to be a bear—a bear had come into town looking for food! I found it highly unlikely that there would be bears in the Palouse, given the fact that the entire area was cultivated—where would they hide? And the Palouse was all dry-land farming with very little water.

I would have never guessed there were bears around, but now I knew to be careful after dark, even around town. I just never would've dreamed there would be bears down in these small eastern Washington towns.

I went to bed, still feeling a bit uneasy, but I soon dropped off to sleep, and I don't recall anything else until my alarm went off at 5 a.m. I always get up before dawn when I'm out doing photography, as my whole reason for being there is primarily to take sunrise and sunset photos.

Even though I was still half asleep, I remembered the figure in the dark. I still felt uneasy, but I needed to turn on the lights. I ended up going into the master wing of the house to get dressed, closing all the doors so the lights wouldn't be noticeable. I decided I would start sleeping back there, as it suddenly felt much more secure.

I was soon on the road again, drinking coffee from my thermos and munching on some granola bars, heading towards a spot that I'd previously determined would make a good place to film the sunrise.

It wasn't that far from town, just a little dirt road that led to the top of the hill where I wouldn't be trespassing in anyone's field. I could set up my tripod and wait for the sun to rise and have a good

360° view, which was rare in the Palouse because of all the rolling hills.

It was a glorious sunrise, and as I took photo after photo, I had a feeling of appreciation for my luck at being able to come to the Palouse and enjoy such beauty. A lot of my photography friends were back in the city, working their day jobs, able to get out only on the weekends. Sure, I was getting older, but I could fortunately still enjoy life.

I drove around more, going back mid-day for a break, then went back to the same hill for the sunset, pointing my camera in the opposite direction.

It was an equally glorious sunset, but with one difference—after it started to get dark, I suddenly felt that same panic I'd felt before, the hair on my neck and arms standing up, with the same urgent sense to flee.

I quickly picked up my photography gear, even though the light was still good and it was turning into the blue hour. I pretty much tossed everything into my car, which was unlike me, as I usually carefully put my expensive gear into its cases.

I drove back down the hill, continually looking in my rear-view mirror, feeling as if something strange was following me. My fear got worse and worse until I was driving pretty recklessly, but once I got back on the highway and could pick up some speed I started to relax a bit.

Once back at the Butcher's House, I parked my car in front, but I felt a strange reluctance to go inside. As I sat there, I realized that I didn't really like the place very much, even though I had tried to, telling Marti that it was a really cool kind of hipster place and that maybe she and her family could come stay with me for a weekend sometime.

The place suddenly felt ominous and even uncomfortable. I sat in the car for a long time, maybe even a half hour or longer, until I finally talked myself into going inside, as there was no point in sleeping in my car when I had a perfectly good bed just a few steps away. It had to be my claustrophobia kicking in—I'd never preferred sleeping in my car to a house.

I moved my stuff into the back master bedroom, where I could keep the door closed and be more private and further away from the front of the house—as well as away from that strange anteroom door.

That night, I had weird nightmares. I haven't had nightmares for many many years, in fact, I can't even remember the last one I had—no, wait, I do recall. It was when I had broken my foot and was on some kind of painkiller, which was years ago.

I finally woke up in a cold sweat, terrified. I'd dreamed that there had been a loud crash and something big had emerged from the door between the house and the butcher shop and had quietly moved through the house, opening the bedroom door and standing over my bed, looking down at me.

And in the dream, even though it was dark, I could make out its huge form, and its glowing red eyes seemed to burn right through me. I was too terrified to move, and the strange odor that I'd smelled in the house now seemed overpowering.

I knew I was going to die in a really bad way as the creature leaned over me, its eyes burning into my skin and its horrible-smelling breath making me want to gag. And just as it raised its massive arm as if to strike, I could hear the sound of a siren coming down the street.

As the siren came closer, the beast turned and fled. I don't know where I got the courage, but I quickly turned on the light. I don't recall waking, and everything seemed to flow together.

There was nothing there, but the strange odor was strong, though I remember thinking it could just be the dream lingering on. I sat up in bed, half afraid to move.

Finally, I picked up my cell phone and looked at the time. It was three a.m.—way too early to get up, and yet I was too frightened to even think of going back to sleep. It suddenly occurred to me that maybe it wasn't a dream, and if so, what if the thing came back?

I slipped on my jeans and shirt, pulled on my hiking boots (forgetting my socks), picked up the big aluminum case that held my camera gear, grabbed my wallet and phone, and slipped out the front door, practically running the short distance to my car.

I jumped in and locked the car doors, then drove away. I had no idea where I was going, but I had to get away from the Butcher's House.

It wasn't until I got to the small town of Palouse that I began to compose myself. I pulled into the post-office parking lot and sat for a while with the car turned off. I'd never felt so disoriented in my life, and I think I was maybe going through a bit of what PTSD must feel like.

After an hour or so, I felt a little better and started to wonder if I might attract attention if a policeman were to drive by, so I pulled out and drove around town a little bit.

I finally drove up the hill above town on the highway that goes to the little town of Garfield, but I stopped just short of the Palouse town limits, not wanting to be alone out in the back country. I was still very spooked.

I pulled off the road under some big trees across from a farm-house, where I sat until I finally dozed off. The next thing I knew, it was dawn. I kind of shook myself awake, then turned around and drove back down the hill into town, hoping to find a cafe open so I could get some coffee and breakfast.

It had been a really harrowing night, but was any of it even real? I mean, why would I have a nightmare and want to run away like that? Don't most people when they have nightmares usually just get up, turn on the lights, wake up a bit, shake it off, then go back to bed? Why had my reactions been so extreme?

I thought about it over a cup of coffee at a little cafe in the center of town, then ordered a good hearty breakfast, dawdling there until it was pretty much daylight. Finally, I paid the bill and went back out to my car, wondering what to do next. I had lost interest in photography, yet it was still really good light, so I decided to drive out by an old stone church that someone had told me about.

I managed to get a few good shots, but after an hour or so I felt really fatigued. I decided to go back to the Butcher's House and get the rest of my stuff and go home.

I would forgo the rest of the week and chalk the cost up to experience. When I'd first seen the listing, I'd noted that it was new and had no reviews. Live and learn, I thought, never rent a place with no reviews.

Once back, the place felt fine, though the odd odor was still there. I decided I might as well hang around until afternoon, do some laundry, upload the photos onto my computer, and then head out in time to maybe get some good sunset shots on the way home, as much as I hated driving after dark. I was anxious to leave, yet wanted to get just a few more evening photos.

As I gathered my clothes, I noticed something on the floor by the bed, something dark and splotchy. I looked closer and found what appeared to be large drops of blood. The strange thing was, the blood was coagulating so wasn't that old, maybe just a few hours or so.

Now, I can tell you that really upset me. Why would there be blood on the floor?

I gathered together the few clothes I had that needed washing and went into the laundry room. The house had a nice front-load washer and dryer that looked almost new. I opened the washer and was ready to toss my clothes in when I noticed there were clothes already inside.

I grabbed a laundry basket and started taking them out, irritated that the owner had neglected to clear out the machine in case I needed it. I was beginning to feel extremely disappointed with the house—I'd expected more, especially for what I'd paid. Sure, they'd said it was their own home, but they should either leave it in better shape or reduce the price.

I started taking the dirty clothes from the washer, but I immediately threw everything back in, then quickly turned and washed my hands thoroughly in the nearby sink.

The clothes were covered in blood, and I knew they must belong to the butcher. Was that also the source of the blood by the bed? It seemed logical, yet the blood by the bed was too fresh.

It was then that I realized that the odd odor I'd been smelling was the faint smell of blood and raw meat. Maybe the butchering was done in the part of the building that was behind the door and the odor was seeping through.

It had seemed so mysterious, but was instead rather disgusting. The owners were used to living with the smell, but I wasn't, and it wasn't my idea of how a nightly rental should smell.

I gathered up my dirty clothes and put them in a plastic trash bag —I would wash everything when I got home. I made a cup of coffee, loaded my stuff, then left, changing my mind about staying until late afternoon. It wasn't even noon, but I couldn't bear to be there any longer.

I can't describe the relief I felt as I drove away, and I decided then and there that I would contact the owners when I got home and ask for a refund for the nights I hadn't stayed. The entire experience had left a bad taste in my mouth, and I knew it would be my last trip to the Palouse, even though the countryside was just as beautiful and nothing had really changed except my own perceptions.

Or was it just me? Was the dream real? Why had the odor of raw meat seemed stronger after my dream? Why was there fresh blood by the bed? Why had I felt the hair on my arms stand up, as well as the urge to flee when out taking sunset photos? Was I losing my mind?

I called Marti on the way back to tell her I was on my way home. She seemed surprised and asked if everything was OK. I really didn't want to talk about it right then, and I told her maybe I would come up to her place for the weekend, if she was OK with that.

She seemed puzzled, but said they would love to have me come up, as it had been a few months. I knew I needed to talk to her and her husband and see if I really was sane or not, as I was beginning to seriously question myself.

I didn't stop anywhere, and I don't think I've ever been so happy to be back in my own house. The security and feeling of safety was almost overwhelming. I almost started crying in relief then unloaded all my stuff, made myself some dinner, and went to bed, exhausted, and slept like a baby.

My questioning of my own sanity pretty much ended the next day when I loaded my photos onto my computer. I actually had little interest in them, and almost felt a sense of dread, but I'm a pretty organized fellow, and I wanted to get them off my camera and delete the bad ones.

As I was flipping through them, now that I could see them better on my big monitor, I got to the ones I'd taken of the sunset up on the hill that night that I'd panicked and jumped in my car.

I was pleasantly surprised with the first photo in that sequence and thought it was pretty darn good, except for a black spot over towards the edge of the photo. I must've had something on the lens, and I told myself that I needed to take better care of my equipment, even though I prided myself on being meticulous.

Looking at the second photo that I took from the hilltop, I noted that the spot seem larger. It was down in a field of yellow wheat not far from where I'd stood to take the photo, and its blackness stood out from the golden background.

Darn it! Were some of the best photos I'd taken on the whole trip ruined by my carelessness? Was it something I could remove with Photoshop?

The third photo also had the black spot in it, but it was a bit larger again. This was beginning to not make any sense. I could understand a spot on the lens, but why would it get progressively larger with each photo?

As I zoomed in on the black spot, I began to feel sick. The spot appeared to be some kind of a creature, something bulky and with large sloped shoulders and long arms that hung down to the top of the wheat stocks. Zooming in even more on what appeared to be its head, I could see two glowing red eyes, and I could barely make out a look on its face that literally gave me the shivers.

I stood up, feeling once again the fear that had haunted me at the Butcher's House, making sure my door was locked and the curtains were pulled, even though it was broad daylight.

I then walked over and shut down my computer, not able to look again at the photo. I paced around the house for a while, trying to regain my composure. Whatever it was, it would be impossible for it to follow me here unless it could travel as fast as an automobile, so it had to still be back in the Palouse.

I made myself a cup of tea and called Marti, asking if I could come up the next day instead of waiting for the weekend, even though I knew they would be at work. I needed to be around other people and figure this out. Marti was very levelheaded, and she would talk me down.

She seemed concerned, but I told her all was well and I would explain once I got there. She only lived a little over an hour away, so it wasn't like I needed to prepare for a long trip. I started my laundry, cleaned up my camera gear a little bit, made a cup of coffee, then went outside and sat on the back porch. I refused to let this thing worry me anymore.

After the fear finally diminished some, I went upstairs and went to bed after watching a little TV. The next day, I went on up to Marti's place, and we had some long talks about what had gone on. I showed her the photos of the black thing, which gave her pause. We both decided that it would be a good idea for me to stay away from the Palouse, not that I wanted to go back.

I'd decided to not contact the owners to ask for a refund, as I basically wanted to forget everything and have nothing more to do with the Butcher's House. But a few days after I got back home from Marti's, I got an email from them asking me to call them.

I really didn't want to have any more contact with them, but I decided to go ahead and see what was going on, as they had said it was urgent. I was worried that they might try to charge me for some kind of damage or for something I hadn't done.

I had emailed them the day I got back home, telling them I'd left, so they knew the house was sitting empty. They'd replied that this was fine, and they would go back early, so I hadn't worried about anything. I made up an excuse of not feeling well, which was actually true, but I didn't tell them why.

Imagine my surprise when they told me that someone had broken into the meat shop before they'd returned and a good portion of a dressed steer was missing. They had a lot of cut and wrapped meat in the cooler, but none of that had been touched.

They were puzzled as to why someone would take the most difficult thing to steal, a heavy steer carcass, as opposed to wrapped meat that would be easier to carry. Carrying a dressed steer was not child's play and would take a couple of strong people.

In addition, the door between the house and the meat shop had the entire handle ripped off. Had I possibly heard or seen anything unusual? Nothing seemed to be missing from the house.

I could feel my hackles rise again. I knew it hadn't been a dream after all, but could I tell them the truth and risk not being believed?

I decided I couldn't, even if they suspected me of the theft. There was no evidence that I had done anything, so I knew I had nothing to worry about.

I simply told them that I hadn't noticed anything amiss when I left. They seemed content with my answer, and that was the last I heard from them.

After thinking about it for awhile, I decided that the creature must've destroyed the handle into the anteroom and come into the house while I'd been sleeping. Perhaps it had a keen sense of smell and and had been attracted to the blood on the clothes in the washing machine, which led it into my bedroom in what I'd thought was a dream. I'd been so distracted and sleep deprived that I hadn't noticed the broken door handle.

This was terrifying enough, but it must have then returned after I'd fled, getting into the meat in the shop and leaving blood on the floor by my bed. I suspected it had come back for me, but not finding me, had stolen the steer carcass.

I've never been one to believe in mysterious things, but now I was a believer—and I had photographic proof, though it probably wasn't enough to convince anyone. The whole experience was kind of what you would call a package deal, and it's one package I don't want to repeat.

I've never been back to the Palouse and instead I now play golf, though I also like fly fishing. I still have all my photo equipment, but

I'm ready to give it to my grandkids. The photo club is disappointed with me dropping out, but they would never believe me if I told them what had happened.

I just tell them I got bored with it all, though that's about as far from the truth as one could get. What really happened there in the Palouse was the opposite of getting bored, and I don't think my aging heart could take another photo encounter of that kind.

2

THE YELLOWSTONE WHISPERS

Winston was part of a group I met while teaching an introductory class in fly-fishing near my home base of Steamboat Springs, Colorado. He was a quiet guy at first, but turned out to be quite a storyteller over the campfire after one of my famous dutch-oven dinners.

Everyone in the group really took to him, and we all listened in rapt silence as he told the following story over the hot coals of the dying fire. Even though we weren't far out in the wilds and fairly close to town, I swear we were half-afraid to leave the firelight when he was done. —Rusty

Well, Rusty, I'm a bit older now, but I was in my 50s when this happened. I'm kind of ashamed to say it took me over half a decade to open my eyes to the world around me, but as they say, better late than never.

The incident I'm about to relate was indeed an eye-opener for me, and I probably learned more about life from it than I did in all my preceding years.

I know you've been to Yellowstone, but a lot of people haven't, and even among those who have, a lot of them don't realize just how huge the place really is.

It's an incredible landscape, very little of which is ever actually visited by people, even by those who get out and hike the back-country trails. There's just so much timber, and a lot of it is so thick you can barely bushwhack your way through it. There's no hunting, and because it's grizzly bear habitat, a lot of people won't hike the interior, and so, it's the perfect habitat for...well, I'll get to that soon.

But my age, that's part of the story. When you get to be middle-aged and you work for a corporation, they often don't see you as an asset, but instead, tend to look at you as someone who is nearing retirement. If they can get rid of you before you retire and qualify for your full pension, they can save a bundle of money.

But they have to do it in a manner that won't come back and bite them on the rear end. They have to make it look like they're down-sizing the company or something like that—they can't be discrimina-tory because of your age—at least in theory, anyway.

To make things worse, I worked in IT as a manager. Computer technology is probably one of the worst jobs you can have these days. It used to be a very secure position, but now you have to stay on top of a lot of new stuff, and it's really easy to give your job to some guy in India. Managers are easy to replace, usually by someone who will work cheaper.

I knew all this, and I knew the writing was on the wall, but I only had two years left until I could retire, and I really hoped I could make it. But the day my manager called me into her office, I had a sinking feeling it was all over, and I was right.

I did manage to negotiate a payout, which wasn't a whole lot. It was about one-half of my annual salary, but it did give me a bit of a buffer until I could figure out what to do next. I would also get a pension, but it wouldn't be much.

What to do? I had no idea, but I knew I needed a change in my life. I was sick of working in a cubicle, and my health had taken a turn for the worse because of my lack of exercise and poor eating habits. I was divorced, no kids, so at least I had no responsibilities except for myself, which was good.

I'll never forget the day I got laid off. I went back to my small apartment and sat there, looking around at the stuff I'd managed to accumulate, kind of in shock.

Twenty-four hours later, that apartment was almost empty. I'd called Habitat for Humanity, who came and took away almost everything to their store. Since that's where I'd gotten most of it anyway, I felt that was appropriate.

I took most of my clothes to the thrift store, as well as my dishes and kitchen stuff. I then went down to the local outdoors store where I told them I was going backpacking in Yellowstone, and I'd soon dropped a nice chunk of change on equipment, which included two canisters of bear spray.

This story is going to be long anyway, so I'll cut to the chase. Forty-eight hours after closing down my apartment, I was in Yellowstone. I don't even remember the drive, except for the emotions I went through, which included shock, bitterness, anger, and excitement.

Why Yellowstone? I'm not really sure. Maybe I'd read it was a good place to get out into the wilderness. I'd never been there, and I had no idea where to go or what to do once I was there.

I couldn't have cared less about seeing the geysers and tourist sites, I was there to run away and hide in the deepest wilderness I could find. I wanted time and space to process everything and decide what to do next. In retrospect, I really had no idea what I was doing. I was being compulsive, I guess, mostly from fear.

But there I was, in Yellowstone National Park. I went into the Visitor Center and got some maps and information and found out that I needed a backcountry permit. This included watching a mandatory video about bear safety. I'd chosen an area of the park where few people go, so it was easy to get a permit.

I didn't know diddly squat about anything, I just knew I needed to get away, even though the ranger I talked to was concerned that I was going out alone, saying that bears are more bold around solo hikers. He said that as a solo backpacker, I really should stay where there were more people, especially since I was new to it all. But I was dead set on being out where there were few people, and I was soon on my way to the trailhead.

Once there, I loaded all my gear into the backpack. The guy at the outdoors store had been really helpful, and I felt like I was pretty much prepared for anything. I had enough freeze-dried food for two weeks, a water filter, rain gear, new boots, and a hammock, which the guy at the store said would be much easier to carry than a tent. I also had a small tarp that I could use if it rained.

All this, along with some cooking gear and a few other things, pretty much made for a full pack—oh, and I even had the required bear-proof storage canister.

Once at the trailhead, I was the only car in the parking lot, which surprised me somewhat, but that's why I was there, because I wanted to get away from people. I will admit that the complete lack of anyone else around made me a bit nervous, as I'd expected to see at least another car or two.

Let me say that I am purposely being vague, as I don't really want to disclose the area where all this happened. I definitely don't want to encourage people to go there, and after reading this account, I know there are people who would try to find where this happened. I don't want to be a part of anyone getting injured, or maybe worse.

I've followed the Yellowstone news since this trip, and I've seen some really odd and mysterious reports, but they are few and far between. I truly think the rangers are trying to keep a lid on all this, and I also think they're probably right to do so. From the talk I had with the ranger at the end of my adventure (or maybe I should call it my misadventure), I can't help but think they know exactly what's going on, even though they probably don't understand it—but I don't think anyone does.

Anyway, I hoisted my pack onto my back and headed up the trail. This was not only my first time backpacking, but it was one of the few times I'd ever gone hiking. Living in the city makes it hard to get very far away, especially when you work all the time, like I had.

I immediately began worrying. What if I ran into a bear? What if I got lost? What if I was so out of shape that I twisted my ankle or worse? At my age, and in as poor condition as I was, even a heart attack could be a possibility. Ironically, I wasn't even aware that the thing that proved to be my greatest danger even existed.

But the further I got up the trail, the more my worries faded away. I was too busy huffing and puffing to worry about anything, as well as trying to adjust my pack so it would stop hurting my shoulders. I moved slow and was soon lost in the beauty around me, the silence broken only by the sound of my own breathing and the call of a pair of ravens.

Ravens. I knew nothing about the species, but I found them intriguing. They followed me, landing in the trees nearby and making all kinds of noise. I found them to be good company, and they made me forget my fears.

Little did I know that ravens aid and abet predators by advertising where prey is, hoping to make good on a free meal after the bear or mountain lion has made the kill and had their fill. If I'd known that, I would've chased them off, thrown rocks at them, whatever it took.

Instead, in my innocence and ignorance, I laughed and felt like I was special for them to pay me so much attention. I later realized how ignorant of the wilds I was, an ignorance that could have easily cost me my life—well, an ignorance that actually almost *did* cost me my life.

The trail didn't climb much, but instead wound through a long beautiful meadow. It was perfect for acclimating myself to the pack and setting a pace. I soon quit huffing and puffing and began to get my stride.

I was in a new world, the most beautiful and primal place I'd ever been. I immediately understood why people became so passionate about nature. I felt sad that I'd spent most of my life in the city. I was in my 50s and only now had discovered how great it felt to get away from it all.

Oh well, I thought, maybe it was for the best. If I'd known about this earlier, I probably would've quit my job and become a guide or something, then so much for having a good retirement.

The irony of it all hit me. I'd pretty much wasted my life, given it to a corporation, and now the only retirement I would have other than my small pension would be social security, and I wouldn't qualify for that for a number of years. I would've been better off in the long run going hiking every day—at least I would be in good shape, which I wasn't now. The thought was discouraging, and I stopped to take a break and sit on a large rock.

I took out a package of M&Ms and ate them as the ravens came near, curious. I almost threw them a few, but I knew it was illegal to feed wildlife in the park, plus I wasn't sure if ravens could eat chocolate—maybe it was poisonous to them, like it was to dogs.

I suddenly wished I had a dog, knowing I'd feel safer, though I knew I wouldn't be able to bring it hiking in the park. Maybe I would get a dog when I got home. It then struck me that I had no home, no place to go.

I sighed. I guessed I would just make Yellowstone my home, at least for the next two weeks. I would deal with the future when I had to. Maybe I'd make the Tetons my next home after this. Then I could call Glacier National Park home for a few weeks.

It gradually dawned on me that I really didn't need a home—I could live out of my car and backpack. I could go south in the winter and north in the summer. It would be a cheap way to live, and I could probably survive on my savings for a couple of years, if not longer, as all I would need was food and gas. Imagine the kind of shape I'd be in!

Maybe I should go to all the parks. That was it! I would spend the next few years trying to visit every national park in the U.S.

I felt energized, maybe from the sugar, but also from the thought of being free. I was soon back on the trail, a spring in my step, my whole outlook changed.

But it didn't take long for the excitement to wane, as I could feel the distance from my car and from civilization with every step, and the worrying soon returned. Keep in mind that I was as unfamiliar with the wilds as a city boy could be, and such unfamiliarity bred hesitation and fear.

I think some fear is probably healthy, as we need to be aware of our surroundings, yet I also recognized that my particular fears were probably misguided, as there was nothing out here that would harm me—other than a grizzly bear or two, maybe.

But suddenly my fears were becoming reality, as I could hear the crunch-crunch sound of something coming down the trail, something really big!

I was terrified and did the opposite of what the Visitor Center movie said to do—instead of making myself known so as to not surprise a bear, I stepped off the trail and hid behind some thick bushes. I knew bears have an incredible sense of smell, but somehow I thought it wouldn't know I was there and would keep on going.

I stood for a moment, scared to death, as sure enough, something really big and dark came down the trail. It paused, then stepped into sight, and I knew it could smell me, for it stopped right next to where I was hidden, swinging its head back and forth and snorting.

A buffalo, or, more accurately, a bison! The thing was huge, and I realized it was probably every bit as dangerous as a bear, maybe even more so. And to make things worse, there were several more behind it!

I tried to reach for my bear spray, but couldn't get to the side pocket in my pack. I realized that this was a real rookie mistake that might cost me my life. All I could do was stand quietly and wait.

After a moment, the bison continued on down the trail, the others following, paying me no mind. I then realized that if it had been a bear, I probably wouldn't have even heard it coming, for bears walk much more quietly.

The bison were soon gone, and I started breathing again, slipped off my pack, put both cans of bear spray in more accessible pockets, then headed back up the trail, feeling shaky.

My first wildlife encounter in Yellowstone had gone pretty well, all things considered. I knew that this would be part of the store of experience that I would gradually build up until I felt more comfortable in the backcountry, and hopefully none of that experience would kill me. I knew that two weeks of this would make me a much more adept and confident backpacker, though I still would be a rookie. Nothing like doing one's first backpack trip in one of the wildest places in America.

I stopped again, resting on a log, wondering how far I'd hiked. I pulled out the map and realized I'd gone maybe a mile at the most. I could already feel my shoulders seizing up from the heavy pack, and my knees were starting to hurt.

At that rate, I'd be lucky to even get a few miles before I'd have to make my first camp. I felt discouraged, but soon realized it just didn't matter. I was free to go when and where I wanted, and if I hiked 100 feet a day, that was fine. I was here to enjoy the wilds and regroup, not set any hiking records. I would start a new life and get in shape along the way.

On the other hand, it was somewhat comforting to know my car wasn't all that far away, so I wasn't really that disappointed to not have gone far.

I was totally alone in the wilds, and I have to admit I was still on edge and fearful. I even toyed with the idea of going back and finding a spot in one of the park's campgrounds, surrounded by people.

But to my credit, I kept going—maybe I wasn't as big of a coward as I'd feared. The ravens had left, and the forest was now very quiet. It began to take on an almost ominous feeling, like before a big storm hits, though the weather forecast had called for good weather.

I instinctively looked to the sky, half expecting to see huge thunderheads forming, but it was a marvelous blue, a color like I'd never seen in the city. In spite of the quiet and tenseness, I felt elated to be there.

I managed to hike another mile or so, then decided it would be prudent to stop for the day and make camp. It was only mid-afternoon, but I was tired, and I knew it would take me awhile to get camp set up, as it was my first time. No reason to push it.

I hadn't seen hide nor hair of another human, which was fine by me. The trail skirted a small meadow, which looked to be perfect for my first camp. There were a few trees that would make a good place to hang my hammock, providing I could remember how to do it.

It felt good to take off the heavy pack, and I soon had the

hammock hung and was resting in it. It was beyond comfortable, and before I knew it, I was waking to a fiery sunset through the trees. I had no idea what time it was, but I knew I'd slept for several hours.

I hurried and set up my little stove and soon had dinner going, a freeze-dried stew with apple crumb for dessert. I was famished and now understood why people said food tasted so much better in the outdoors. I was also very thirsty and drank one of the four water bottles I carried. I wasn't worried about refilling it, as the ranger had said water was plentiful in this area. I would have to filter whatever I found, but it was no big deal.

Now with a restful nap and dinner behind me, I felt much better, and I was soon leaning back in the hammock watching the stars come out.

I'll never forget that first night out—it was so incredibly beautiful and peaceful. Later, after what I went through, I would often remember how that first night out was so different from what was to come.

But then, ignorance is bliss, as they say.

The Greater Yellowstone Ecosystem is one of the wildest and least-touched places in the U.S. In my ignorance, I had no idea that unknown creatures could exist there, unnoticed and undetected. I think that next time I'll go to someplace less remote to find myself— but I'm getting ahead of the story.

Even though I'd slept for several hours, I was still exhausted, but I wanted to stay awake to enjoy the starry sky. I knew it would be a sight like I'd never seen before and would include my first time seeing the Milky Way. But I was soon fast asleep, dead to the world around me, which may not have been so wise given where I was.

We humans can't see very well in the dark, so it's important that we're protected as best can be at night, especially when sleeping in a hammock, which is actually quite exposed—at the very least, one should have a headlamp and bear spray handy. I had neither, leaving both in my pack.

But I guess my senses were still on partial alert, as something did wake me, though I had no idea what—I just knew I was suddenly wide awake from a deep sleep.

I lay very still, listening, but all was quiet. I finally decided I'd awakened because I'd forgotten to put my food in the bear canister. I fumbled around and found my headlamp, put my food away, and tidied camp a bit, then climbed back into my hammock, tucking my headlamp and bear spray into the hammock's side pocket. The slight swaying soon made me nod off again, but it was short-lived, as I again awoke.

I'd heard something, but what? It had to be a strange noise to wake me, but then, everything out here was a strange noise to my city ears. Once again, I lay still, listening, but now getting more and more fearful. What if it was a bear? I slowly pulled out the bear spray and held it ready.

Now I could hear what sounded like children laughing, though far in the distance. I wasn't that far from the trailhead, and perhaps a young family had hiked in behind me and camped nearby.

And even though it seemed odd that young children would be up in the middle of the night, it gave me a sense of comfort, knowing there were others nearby. Soon, the laughter faded into the distance, turning into a whispering sound as if the wind was moving through the forest. I soon fell back asleep.

I woke at dawn, the bear spray resting on my chest, tiny birds flitting around and chirping in the trees above. It took awhile to wake up, and I first thought I was back in my apartment and couldn't make sense of anything, especially the birds, but I eventually realized where I was.

I was soon up, making coffee and a freeze-dried packet of scrambled eggs. I was again famished, and I followed the eggs down with two granola bars and some raisins, then made yet another package of eggs.

Man, at this rate, I would run out of food in a week. I would just have to be sure I didn't get too far out so I could return in short order if I needed to, though at the speed I was going, that wouldn't be much of a concern.

I lazed around in my hammock, sore but happy. I was in the most beautiful of places, and the worries of the previous day were forgotten, though I still wondered why children would be playing during the night.

It was mid-morning before I had my pack ready and again hit the trail. Today I would keep an eye out for water, as I'd already used half of what I was carrying. I would also keep an eye out for the family I'd heard during the night, as it would be nice to see others out here. Maybe I could even hike with them a ways.

I found I was almost too sore to continue, but as the day wore on, I kind of walked it out and felt better, though I did stop a lot to rest. Once again, my appetite got the better of me, and I stopped mid-day to make a packet of freeze-dried spaghetti. So much for losing all my flab, though I knew I was burning a lot of calories.

I never did see the family I'd heard during the night, and as I got deeper and deeper into the wilds, I vacillated between pure elation and sheer panic. Fortunately, the elation usually won out, and the feelings of panic gradually subsided.

I felt like I was getting used to this new life, this new wilderness environment, the one we humans had originally called home long before we habituated ourselves to city life like a bunch of scurrying ants.

Before long, just like the ranger had predicted, I came upon a small stream. I stopped and filtered water, which took much longer than I had anticipated. I then continued on up the trail until I could see what looked like steam rising through the trees. I knew I had to be nearing some of Yellowstone's thermal activity.

Although Yellowstone is famous for its large geysers, such as Old Faithful, a lot of the park is dotted with hot pools and small geysers. These are a delight to the numerous bison and other wildlife during the winter, as the heat helps mitigate the extremely cold temperatures in the park. In the summer, the hot pools are a delight to people like myself, who enjoy bathing their tired aching bodies in the water, as long as it's not too hot.

I veered off-trail and headed towards the steam, excited. I was so sore that the thought of dangling my feet in warm water sounded heavenly.

Sure enough, I was soon at several hot pools with a small stream running through them. I hoped the stream would mellow out the boiling thermal waters enough to bathe in.

I quickly had my boots off and was soaking my feet in the warm water. It was indeed heavenly. Even though I hadn't come more than a few miles, I knew this would be my next camp.

I was soon stripped-down and immersed up to my neck in the warm waters, feeling like I'd found paradise, my sore muscles relaxing.

So far, I was thoroughly enchanted with Yellowstone. My city woes were far behind, and I would've been hard pressed to tell you even what city I'd lived in, though it hadn't been that long ago.

I spent the entire rest of the day there, finally forcing myself to get out of the water before I wrinkled up, it felt so good. I found a couple of trees that were perfect for my hammock, then got out my cooking gear. Still hungry, I made myself another dinner, following that with a hot cup of tea and an apple.

It was now evening, and I noticed movement in the trees beyond the small meadow with the hot pools. There was something dark back in there, and I reached for my bear spray. Before long, the dark figures had moved out from the forest to where I could see them.

Once again, it was bison, a small group of six, and I knew they wanted to come to the water. They seemed wary because I was there, for they stood looking in my direction. I decided to walk back into the woods a ways, giving them space enough to come and drink.

Still carrying the bear spray, I slipped back into the trees, pushing my way through thick undergrowth until I came upon an animal trail that wound through the forest.

Near the trail was a small clearing in the undergrowth, and I soon realized that it was probably a place where bears bedded down during the day. I was instantly on alert, and even more so when I saw several large bear tracks on the trail ahead of me. They were the first

I'd ever seen, and I marveled at how large they were, though I couldn't help but shiver.

I decided I should go back to camp, as the last thing I wanted was an encounter with a grizzly. But as I turned around, I saw something quickly slip off the trail into the trees. It had been no more than 30 feet behind me! I felt a surge of adrenaline.

Whatever it was, it was large and dark, so I figured it was a black bear. It certainly was quiet, I noted as I pushed my way back through the undergrowth in panic, making lots of noise. The Visitor Center movie had talked about how fast bears can run, but it hadn't said anything about a bear following someone, especially so quietly.

I stopped at the edge of the forest to check on the bison, which were now drinking from the stream, but they suddenly turned and stampeded.

Had I frightened them? It didn't seem likely, as I hadn't yet stepped from the trees where they could see me. Bison have a reputation for being fearless, and I'd read about a woman who'd been stomped to death by one in Teddy Roosevelt National Park. Yellowstone tourists also frequently had encounters with them, occasionally fatal. I was actually surprised that my presence earlier had made them fearful enough to not come to the stream.

I then realized that the bear that I'd seen on the trail had probably frightened the herd. Would a bear cause them to stampede like that? Something didn't feel quite right. Were bison really that afraid of bears? Were there hunters around? No, it wasn't the right time of year, and besides, there's no hunting in national parks.

I thought it would probably be prudent to move camp, especially seeing how close I was to a bear trail, but I was just so exhausted that doing so didn't seem possible. Soaking in the hot water had turned me into a limp noodle, and I'd already been tired when I'd arrived.

The thought was too much, so I tidied up camp, then crawled into my sleeping bag in my hammock to watch the sunset, too tired to worry about much.

The sunset was fiery beyond anything I'd ever seen, yet I was too fatigued to even get my camera out for a photo.

I drifted off, tired to the bone, but again awoke in the middle of the night to children's laughter. As before, it seemed distant, so I listened for awhile, then went back to sleep, thinking the family was again nearby. It made sense that they would be progressing up the trail at about my speed if they had young children with them. Why they were so noisy at night was beyond me, but I was soon back asleep.

I suddenly woke in a panic. I felt as if I were in the middle of a circle of strange creatures all whispering at once, whispering loud like the wind. My hammock began swaying, and the rational part of my mind said it had to be the wind, though I somehow knew it was the strange creatures.

And as I lay there, my hammock swaying more and more, I remembered reading long ago about the Yellowstone Whispers. Try as I might, I couldn't remember much besides that people would hear a strange whispering sound in Yellowstone, even though it would be a calm day or night.

But now something was trying to strangle me! I could feel huge hands around my neck holding me down, trying to cut off my air. And now the whispering grew even louder. I began struggling, and the hands let go.

Now my hammock stopped swaying, the whispering stopped, and I began to realize it was a dream, even though it felt real. I lifted myself up and looked around. There was nothing there.

I could see it was morning, and I was surrounded by a thick fog, my down sleeping bag soaked to the gills. Wet and chilly, I swung from my hammock and quickly pulled the tarp from my pack, trying to make a shelter, but soon gave up. It was too late, everything was already wet.

Even though I wasn't very outdoors savvy, I knew I was in trouble, for the guy at the outdoors store had told me that wet down has absolutely no insulating power.

I did have enough sense to pull my dry clothes from my pack and change before I got chilled, putting on a fleece hoodie under my rain jacket and rain pants. I was now warm and dry, but my sleeping bag wasn't going to be much use unless the sun came out soon, which didn't look likely.

A feeling of desolation and hopelessness set in. I was still in shock from dreaming I was being strangled—it had seemed so real. I felt disoriented and afraid.

I sat for some time in the wet forest, on edge, trying to figure out what to do. I finally decided I should leave, though doing so felt like failure to me—I knew I'd come unprepared. I should be carrying a tent for inclement weather like this, or at the very least a waterproof cover fitted to my hammock.

A better outdoorsman could have probably made it all work, but I had no idea how to set up the tarp so it would keep me dry while in a hammock.

I managed to stuff everything into my pack, then turned and headed back down the trail, feeling the entire time like I was being watched and even possibly followed. I recalled the dark creature I'd seen behind me on the trail the previous day, and as time wore on, it felt like it was back. It was truly the creepiest feeling I've ever experienced.

It also seemed really strange that such bad weather had come in so quickly in spite of what the ranger had said about the forecast. It just didn't make sense.

But I hadn't walked more than a half mile when the sun broke through, and I was once again under blue skies. I turned and looked back from where I'd come, and I could see a blackish-blue fog covering everything, a thick bank enveloping the distance, so strange and so abrupt. The sky in all other directions was clear.

I now felt fairly normal, the creepy feeling almost gone, though I was still on edge. Yet it still somehow felt like my very survival was being challenged, and I knew I had to get out of there as quickly as possible. I wondered again about the family whose kids I'd heard, and I hoped they were okay.

I hitched my pack up onto my back and around my hips, getting it settled, when I felt a strange constriction around my neck, as if I were getting a bad sore throat. I instinctively touched it and was surprised to find that it felt very sensitive, as if bruised.

The dream flashed back, and I now wondered if it had indeed actually happened. A strange sense of terror flowed over me, something I'd never felt in my life, making me want to run recklessly down the trail.

I turned back one last time to look at the fog bank, only to find with horror that it was quickly coming my way, slithering along like a huge dark snake.

I turned back to the trail and ran as fast and as hard as I could, pack bouncing against my back, even though I'd snugged it down tightly.

It's difficult to run with a large pack, and my instincts said to ditch it so I could go faster, but my sense of survival said I might need its contents, as I was several long miles from the trailhead, a distance that had taken me two days to hike.

Of course, I was taking my time back then, but there was no way I could return all that much quicker. And even though I was now running, I wasn't in shape to run far—in fact, I was already getting a hitch in my side.

I had to slow down to a fast walk, and I made the mistake of looking behind me, only to see the fog bank even closer. My running had been for naught.

I tried to find a pace that would allow me to move along quickly without getting winded, but I was just too out of shape. I was now panting. I had to stop and take a break, though it was the last thing I wanted to do.

As I stood on the trail, bent over, sides heaving, the fog caught up with me. I could see its dark tendrils creeping around my ankles and feet, and it felt cold and sticky. The panicky feeling of being watched also returned. I could also now smell a strange sickly-sweet odor, kind of like sulphur and pine pitch mixed together. But worst of all, I could hear the children laughing in the distance, laughter that soon faded into a deep whispering that seemed to filter through the trees and shrubs and into my very being.

I again took off running, but the fog was moving too fast, and there was no way I could outrun it. I was soon totally enveloped to the point that I could barely make out the trail.

I knew it was critical that I stay oriented, but it was getting darker and darker by the moment, and I almost felt like I was being overtaken by night.

As I reached to pull out my headlamp, I caught my toe on a tree root in the trail and went down hard, landing on my right knee. The pain was excruciating, and as I lay underneath my heavy pack, my quiet life flashed before me, my life working in a cubicle in the city, and I wanted nothing more than to be back there.

My grand plan to create a new life was crashing down all around me, and even worse, I somehow feared this Yellowstone adventure could be my first and last.

Nothing made sense anymore. Why had I heard children laughing during the night? How could the sound turn into a whispering? What had been behind me when I was on the bear trail? Whatever it was, it was scary enough to frighten bison. Who had tried to strangle me? And why did this fog seem so malevolent?

I had to be losing my mind. I'd spent so much time in the city, being indolent and lazy, that my poor brain couldn't process things going on in the natural world.

I slipped my pack off and managed to pull myself up, using a nearby small tree for leverage. Gingerly putting weight on my knee, it seemed like it would hold me, even though it was sore. I decided that I'd probably cracked or bruised the kneecap. I had to continue on.

I figured I'd probably come a mile at that point, maybe even further. I had no idea how far it was back to my car, but I estimated at least another two or three miles.

I hoisted my pack back on and found that I was able to walk, though slowly, and I had to be very careful. If there was something after me, it looked like I didn't stand a chance.

It was then that I remembered the bear spray. I pulled both cans from my pack and stuck them in the pockets of my rain jacket. I would at least go down fighting.

As I hobbled along, I knew I had no choice but to keep going, no matter what. Even if things hadn't been so weird, there was no way I could spend the night in the damp and cold without a warm sleeping bag. I had no choice but to get back to my car, even if it was after dark. And, in all honesty, there was no way I wanted to spend another night out there.

I stopped and got a water bottle and some gorp and several ibuprofen from my pack. I would continue on as best I could, and maybe these things would help.

The fog was thick, and I had to watch carefully so I didn't trip again or even lose the trail completely. It couldn't be any later than about noon, but it was so dark I could barely make my way. But fortunately, the pain in my knee seemed to be abating somewhat, the ibuprofen helping.

I don't know how long I continued, lost in the pain and fog, but it seemed like hours. I stumbled along, barely able to make out the trail, my mind lost in thoughts of my past life and pondering how I got where I was.

For some strange reason, I flashed on a memory, something I hadn't thought about for a long time. I recalled standing and looking out the window of my little rental house, watching as a police car pulled up next door.

My neighbor was kind of a straggly burned-out fellow who spent a lot of time working on his old car. He was outside, looking under the hood, and didn't see the two policemen drive up. They startled him, and as he jumped, they grabbed him, frisked him, then put handcuffs on him and took him away.

I never did find out what he was wanted for, but I never saw him again. After a few weeks, someone came and cleaned out his house, taking all his stuff away, and eventually someone else moved in.

Why I remembered this while out on the trail I don't know, but for some reason I began to feel like it would've been better had they come and taken *me* away instead. I would be better off in jail than out here losing my mind. For some reason, that's how afraid I was, that I would prefer to be in jail than stumbling down that trail in Yellowstone.

I was fatigued, and I couldn't even make out the forest I was walking through, the fog was so thick. I could only assume I was going the right way, as the trail seemed to be gradually going downhill. I still had no idea how far it was to my car.

I'd lost track of all time—in fact, I felt as if I had no sense of time at all—everything was timeless, time no longer existed. I had to be sleepwalking, yet I knew I was awake because my knee was killing me, and my neck was so sore I could barely turn my head.

To make things even worse, every so often I could hear the whispers come and surround me, just like in my dream. For some reason, I knew I couldn't let on that I was afraid, and after awhile, I even started yelling at them and telling them to go away. I truly felt that I had lost my mind.

After what seemed like forever, I wondered if I were maybe in a dream, a dream where I would be on this long treacherous walk forever, unable to stop, walking on and on.

Just when I thought things couldn't get any worse, well, that's when I heard it. I could hear a scuffling noise coming up behind me, and I wondered if it weren't the bison again. But for some reason I knew it wasn't, perhaps because of the feeling which had returned, an almost supernatural terror of the unknown.

I desperately wanted to run as I heard the heavy footsteps getting closer behind me, but it was all I could do to stumble along. Finally, when whatever it was sounded as if it were right behind me, I decided to turn and face it.

If I were going to die, I would at least die knowing what had killed me, though I somehow knew it wasn't a bear. And when I turned to face it, I immediately wished I hadn't.

What I saw was like nothing I could ever begin to describe, a creature so horrible and terrifying that even trying to remember it makes me want to blank out. At the time, I had no idea what it was, though now I think I do.

It was the legendary Bigfoot, but not like anything I'd ever read about, not like the Bigfoot that disappears into the woods after you see it, or comes into your camp and makes a lot of noise.

It was something much more elemental—more like the true essence of Bigfoot, a creature that goes beyond all mythology and that has evolved through time, becoming more and better adapted to an environment that is as wild as the beast itself—the primal and fiery landscape of Yellowstone.

It had nothing benign about it, and the moment I saw it, I knew its intentions were to kill me. I flashed back to feeling the huge hands around my neck, and I knew now it wasn't a dream. What I didn't know was why it hadn't killed me, why it had stopped, for it could have easily snapped my neck with one movement. I'll never know, but it seemed to have something to do with the whispers.

Instantly, I felt like I was dealing with the supernatural, and I felt as if I were suspended in time and space, that I had shifted from my own reality into another.

But when the giant creature lunged at me, I brought both cans of bear spray up at the same time, hitting the triggers, and a dense fog of capsaicin enveloped it. I knew bear spray would have no effect on something supernatural, and yet the Bigfoot immediately grabbed for its eyes and lurched backwards.

It screamed a sound like nothing I'd ever heard before, a sound that still wakes me in the middle of the night in sheer terror.

There was nothing I could do. I couldn't run, but now I could again hear the whispers all around me, louder and more intense, as the creature fell back in pain. And now, the whispers seemed protective, like they were surrounding me in order to help me.

I turned and hobbled on as best I could down the trail, expecting to be grabbed from behind at any instant. I'd read about the horrors of dying from a bear, and I wondered if death by Bigfoot would be as gruesome. Would anyone ever find my body? Would I become just another missing person statistic?

I could now hear the whispers fading into the distance like a flock of birds, and for some reason, the fog seemed to drift away back behind me. I was soon walking in broad daylight again, though it looked to be late afternoon, as the shadows were lengthening.

After awhile, I stopped to eat a few handfuls of gorp and drink some water, as I could feel my energy seriously lagging. The fog was now a distant dark line far away in the trees.

I thought again of the bear spray, which had obviously worked, which meant that the Bigfoot was real—and this also meant that once it recovered, it would be even angrier, wanting even more to come after me. And this time, with no bear spray to fend it off, I would be doomed.

I had to get to my car, and soon. I felt very disoriented and didn't recognize anything along the trail, and had no idea how far away the trailhead was. I wasn't even sure I was on the right trail anymore.

I have since learned to stop and look back when I'm hiking so things look familiar when I'm returning, but at that time it was just another of my rookie mistakes to not orient myself better.

I stumbled on for another half hour or so when I saw something on the trail ahead of me. I panicked for a moment, then realized I was looking at fellow humans. The emotions I felt were indescribable.

It was a ranger and two young men, and when they saw I was injured, they offered to help me back to my car. They'd been out searching for a couple who'd gone missing several days earlier.

Fortunately, my car was less than a half mile away, and with one of the guys carrying my pack, we made good time, getting back just as it was getting dark.

I was never so happy to see my car! But there was one minor problem, which was that I couldn't drive with my knee messed up, so one of the guys drove me back to the nearest campground, where the others met us and helped set up camp.

I thanked them profusely, and after we made some small talk, the ranger asked if anything odd had happened while I was out backpacking. I told him about the fog and the whispers, but I decided not to mention the Bigfoot lest they all think I was truly crazy. The ranger said something about the Yellowstone Whispers being quite famous, though he'd never heard them himself. He hesitated, as if he wanted to say more, but they all finally left, as it was late.

After making dinner, I climbed into my hammock, happy to be surrounded by people, and tried to go to sleep. I kept opening my eyes and looking at all the people around me in tents, RVs, and pickup campers, and I felt very happy that I was there, safe and secure.

But I had hoped too soon for peace and quiet. I awoke sometime in the middle of the night again in terror, once again feeling those big hands around my neck. I managed to twist around in my hammock and fall to the ground, which woke me.

I wasn't hurt, but I did know that this time it was a dream, and I grabbed my sleeping bag and spent the rest of the night sleeping on the backseat of my car, doors securely locked. It would be the last time I ever slept in a hammock.

The next day, I was still in a lot of pain, but I was now able to drive, so I decided to go up north to the town of Livingston and see a doctor. I went into the emergency room, where they told me I had indeed cracked my kneecap, but there was little they could do for me except give me a prescription for painkillers and advise me to stay off it.

The doctor noticed the red marks around my neck and examined them with concern, asking what had happened. I just made up a bogus story about getting into a fight in a bar, and he let it go at that, telling me to put Neosporin on the places where the skin had been abraded.

Afterwards, I checked into a comfy motel there for a few days, resting and mulling over everything that had happened. Every night, I would dream that I was being choked and would wake up in a dry sweat. And when evening came, I had to fight the urge to flee, to hit the road and go back to the city, any city.

There was something about nightfall that made me restless and unsettled. But the worst was when I would wake in the night hearing the scream of the creature.

One evening, as I was hobbling back and forth in the room,

forcing myself to not run away, it dawned on me just how close I still was to Yellowstone.

Livingston is only about an hour from the north gate, and even though I'd backpacked more in the southern end of the park, all that wilderness was a simple hour away. Actually, it was even closer, for Livingston is surrounded by mountains that are home to grizzlies and wolves—and most likely Bigfoot. The wilderness was almost right out my door.

I now felt like I was having a mental breakdown. I had to get a grip on myself. What about my plans to see all the national parks? Wilderness was part of the definition of a national park, and if I couldn't deal with the wilds, I might as well go back to the city, get another job, and go ahead and gradually die from inactivity and boredom.

Was that what I wanted? In a way, I felt like I was suffering from PTSD. Maybe I needed to see a therapist. But who would believe such a story? I would probably end up being committed.

But I had to talk to someone. I recalled the look the ranger had given me as he left after we had discussed the fog and the Yellowstone Whispers. I had the distinct feeling that he knew I'd left something out.

Maybe I should go back down to the park and talk to him, but the thought of going back into Yellowstone gave me the shivers. What if my car broke down and no one came around to help me out in the middle of nowhere?

I thought about it long and hard, then realized that with the millions of visitors there every year, my fears of no one to help were irrational. I would go back the next day.

It took awhile to track the ranger down, but I finally found him in the same campground where I'd fallen from my hammock. He seemed surprised to see me, and asked if I'd checked back in with the Visitor Center to let them know I'd come out.

I told him that I hadn't realized I was supposed to, and he said he would call and and let them know. The last thing they wanted was another search in the park.

He invited me to sit down at a picnic table with him and share a cold soda. He then got to talking about the missing couple, who they still hadn't found. Had I seen or heard anything unusual? The last place they'd been seen was on the same trail I'd come down.

I once again got the feeling he wanted to ask me something, yet was hesitant to do so. I told him I hadn't heard or seen any other people.

I recalled the children's laughter in the night. Would that have anything to do with the missing couple? Should I tell him about it?

The ranger then asked me how my knee was doing, and I told him it was cracked. He asked how I'd managed to fall hard enough to crack my kneecap, and I told him I'd been running. He looked at me really funny, and asked if I'd been running from something or somebody, maybe the same somebody who had left the black bruises around my neck.

It was then that I knew he was aware of strange happenings, and I decided to tell him everything. After all, I'd come down expressly to talk to him, and I needed to clear the air and see what he might know.

It took some time for me to get it all out, as it sounded so outlandish, but I could tell from the look on his face that he believed me. When I was finished, he simply looked at me and said, "Do you realize how lucky you are?"

I replied, "Lucky? My first backpacking trip ever and something tries to kill me? I don't think I could've picked a worse place, nor been so unlucky."

The ranger replied, "Nobody understands the whispers, though many have heard them. It's one of the great mysteries of the park. They were first reported by early explorers, mostly in the vicinity of Yellowstone and Shoshone lakes. But even fewer have seen what we call the Yellowstone Fog. The fog isn't something you want to see, for those who have seen it have typically had encounters with a very malevolent creature. Nobody knows what causes the fog, but some think it's related to the same intricate underground system that causes the geysers and hot springs."

He continued, "None of the rangers will discuss this in public. There's no reasoning behind it, though some think the creature lives where the fog is prevalent and uses it as a cover. How the whispers are involved is a true mystery."

"But back to being lucky. This is not anything I want you to repeat, but we have found a number of missing people in areas where the fog has also been seen, and several have been dead from broken necks. That's what I mean when I say you don't realize how lucky you are. The ones who have survived have told the same story you just told me. I'm worried to death that we'll find that missing couple the same way."

I asked, "Do you think the creature heard the couple and left me right as it was getting ready to kill me?"

"Anything's possible. It would explain it, but who knows why the creature didn't kill you. It may have had something to do with the whispers. But I will tell you that a number of rangers have seen Bigfoot, and one nicknamed Action Jackson has even written in print about his encounters—he was a highly respected ranger in his day."

We talked for a long time, and it was dark when I drove on back through the park and back to Livingston. I was surprised at my courage to drive in the dark through the park, but it really wasn't too bad.

I was anxious to get back to my room and away from the wilds, even though I saw a beautiful Great Horned Owl in my headlights on the way back. I also got to see the Milky Way through my windshield, as I was too scared to get out to really look at it. Even through glass, it was the most incredible sight I've ever seen—well, almost anyway. I think the creature will always hold that dubious honor.

It's very unlikely that I'll ever backpack again, but I will go hiking, though not alone. I've been back to Yellowstone since then, but mostly just to see the geysers, and I stayed in places with lots of tourists around. Oh, and I learned later that the couple was found, safe and sound, fortunately.

Not long after all this happened, I came to grips with my fears and realized I would never be the same. I would never be able to sleep out under the stars and feel comfortable. So, I bought a small RV and now travel with friends when I can, though I do sometimes go alone.

At the time of this telling, I've seen 22 of the parks, and I'll soon be on my way to Alaska to see the ones there. Talk about wilderness! But I'm traveling with friends, so I'm not going anywhere out there alone. And I now have two wonderful rescue dogs who are my lifetime buddies and who make me feel safe at night.

I learned a lot about nature and myself on that ill-fated backpacking trip, and I have the utmost respect for the natural world and my place in it. I know I'll never be a seasoned outdoorsman, and that's okay, for I've learned my limits and what I feel comfortable with. And I've also learned that there are things out there that we know very little about.

Personally, I'm happy to keep it that way.

3

THE PARADIGM SHIFT

I met Professor McClurg down on the Bitterroot River just out of the small town of Darby, Montana. I'd stopped at a fishing access site there and saw him out in the water in waders, apparently not having much luck.

When he finally came to the bank, we talked a bit, and I gave him a couple of flies that I thought would work better than what he was using. One of them was my own creation, what I call a Woolly Bigfoot, but I noticed he got kind of quiet when I told him that.

It wasn't long before I'd coaxed him into telling me the following story. It's kind of long, but I found it very interesting, and more than a bit intimidating. —Rusty

You're familiar with what a paradigm shift is, aren't you, Rusty? You know, when your outlook on something completely changes and you don't see it the same way at all anymore?

Well, that's what I think happens to people when they see Bigfoot, their whole lives go through a paradigm shift. I think it's easier on people from the cities than it is for someone who's lived their whole life in the outdoors. I think hunters and campers and outdoors people are the ones most affected and are the ones who probably suffer the most.

I mean, you basically grow up thinking the only dangers in the outdoors are maybe bears and mountain lions, depending on where you live, or maybe a rattlesnake or two. But these are all things that everyone agrees exist, and you can find pictures of them and even talk to people who've had encounters with them, and you know how to deal with them.

To suddenly realize that there's a large hominid-like creature out there and that you're no longer the only bipedal-type creature in the wilds, and not only that, but that this creature is intelligent and cunning and could rip you from limb to limb without even trying, well, it creates a major shift in how you see the world.

Like a lot of other people who have seen Bigfoot, I can say it forever changed my life, and in some ways it made me realize that our planet is much more mysterious than I'd ever thought, which gave me a greater sense of awe and wonder.

But the flip side of that was it left me with a very deep and raw feeling of discomfort, like I'm no longer safe in the outdoors, unless I'm in a place that other people go, like a fishing access close to town. And given that I'm an archaeologist and spend a lot of my time outside, well, this is no minor thing, especially since I chose my profession partly because it would get me out of the office.

Even though my story happened over 10 years ago, I still wake some nights in a cold sweat with nightmares, and I know I can never regain my sense of innocence as a human being at the top of the chain of life. We're taught that humans are the highest form of intelligence on Earth, but I no longer believe it's true.

So, on with the story. I'm hesitant to use the word story, because it makes it sound like I made it all up, but it happens to be true. I think telling it to you will help me process it better, which is one reason I'm willing to talk about it.

OK, fast forward or maybe I should say rewind into a time in my career when I wanted to make a big discovery. Part of that is the publish or perish syndrome in academia, but an even bigger part was my own hubris, wanting to make a difference in my profession. You see, I had grand plans for my career as an archaeologist.

I was an assistant professor at that time, which basically means you don't have tenure and pretty much are still in the process of proving yourself. Once you do have tenure and become a full professor, you can relax somewhat because you now have a secure job.

Jobs in academia are not easy to get, so it can be pretty brutal. This particular archaeological dig I'm going to discuss brought me the tenure I'd been wanting, but the price I paid was extremely high. It made me frequently feel mentally unstable, which eventually cost me my marriage.

My specialty at the time was arctic archaeology. I would rather not mention the university I'm affiliated with, for obvious reasons, but I will say that it's not in Alaska. Most of my research up until then had been done in the coastal areas of southwest Alaska, but I had been involved with other digs, particularly one in northwest Alaska that I will mention later, as I think there may be a connection.

The project that brought me tenure was not an extremely old site as archaeology goes, only about 400 years before present, or about 1600 A.D.

This was a period when the Little Ice Age was encroaching on Alaska, making life very difficult. Food was extremely scarce, and the native peoples began fighting with one another for their survival, raiding villages, killing each other, and stealing food.

The native Alaskan Yupik people have oral traditions about this period, which archaeologists call the Bow and Arrow Wars, when entire villages were destroyed. The dig I worked on was from that period and in southwest Alaska.

This project, which I led, resulted in the best preserved Yupik artifact collection ever found. It was significant and, all in all, it also made my reputation and resulted in my getting the tenure I wanted, just as I ironically lost interest in arctic archaeology and switched to archaeology of the American southwest.

The large sod house I partially excavated, along with a number of students and volunteers, had once held what was probably an extended family of around 30 people. Someone had attacked the village, catching its inhabitants by surprise. I originally thought the attack was by a nearby group of Yupik, but that theory later changed, as you'll see.

What remained was a perfect snapshot of Yupik life, for everything had been left just as it had been when the villagers were killed, for that period in time was extremely cold and the artifacts were very well preserved. We found all kinds of items used in daily life, as well as tools and hunting implements.

But there's a part of the story that very few are aware of, a part that included proof that the neighboring Yupik were not involved in the killing. That discovery led to me shutting the dig down, though only a few know the real reason.

But I shut everything down for two reasons—my reputation was at stake, as well as the lives of everyone involved. It was a decision based first on safety, and second on the fact that no one would believe what was going on even if they saw my proof. I made the decision that some things are better left alone, and I believe it was the right thing to do.

While I was back home trying to recover from what I'd seen at the site, a huge storm came in from the Bering Straits and washed away over 100 feet of shoreline which included the sod house, erasing forever one of the most terrifying past events one can imagine—a past event that looked like it might be repeated if we didn't get the heck out of there.

But let me start at the beginning. I came into my office one day to find a voice message from a professor at a university in Alaska. That particular professor was well-known in arctic archaeology, and we had collaborated on several digs, so we knew each other well.

He asked me to call him, saying that he had something that might be of interest. I was soon on the phone, discussing a call he'd received from one of the elders of the Yupik tribe. I'll call this professor Dave, even though that's not his real name.

This elder told Dave about what could prove to be a significant site. The nearby village had known about this site for years, but some of the villagers were against having archaeologists come in. Their oral tradition said that it was an ancient Yupik village that had been decimated by something, possibly neighboring Yupik during the Bow and Arrow Wars.

The village was basically a large structure dug about four feet into the ground that had been framed by spruce beams and poles. The roof and walls were sod, and inside were various rooms, with a fire-place in one large central room. It appeared to be the dwelling of one large family, or clan.

Well, it appears that the site was in danger of being eroded away by the sea, so this particular elder had finally talked the village into getting someone in there to try to preserve the cultural items from their ancestors. Because the site was in tundra, it had been remark-ably preserved, but the tundra was melting and priceless cultural items were washing away.

"There's more to the story," Dave said, as we talked. "The Yupik aren't particularly superstitious, but few will go near the old village, saying it's haunted by evil spirits. Some have even claimed to have seen spirits walking around the old village, and a few have even claimed they were chased while on snowmachines in the area."

"What do these supposed spirits look like?" I asked. "Can you think of a logical explanation for it all?"

"The elder and I didn't get into that kind of detail," Dave answered. "But I've heard these kind of stories before, and they seem to be common all over Alaska with the natives. Who knows, but maybe there's something to them. But the main thing here is that we have a village washing away, and the natives have invited us to come in and excavate it before it's too late. Do you think your people would be interested?"

"Why aren't you guys doing it?" I asked.

"We're up to our eyeballs in other digs in similar situations," Dave replied. "And as you know, just like everyone else, we have limited funding. You guys have such a good reputation doing this kind of archaeology that it was unanimous that we should offer it to you."

I told Dave I would take it to our research committee, if he could send me more information. And to make a long story short, due to the urgency of the situation, we had a team put together, funds secured, and the dig started within just a few months, which is unheard of, at least at my university. Such things can typically take a year or two.

I can't begin to tell you how excited I was. I'd managed to convince several of my graduate students to go along for what would probably be an entire season in southwest Alaska, which would be about six weeks, as that's about the only real window you get with good weather in those parts.

In addition, we had gathered a number of seasoned volunteers, people who had lots of experience, even though they weren't archae-ologists. Some of our volunteers were retired and more than happy to pay their own expenses just so they could be involved in something like this. We also had a few undergraduate students, all eager to get some field experience.

We were all soon on the shore of Bristol Bay, not far from the Arolik River, with the Alaska Peninsula defining the views to our southwest. I knew Kodiak Island with the town of Kodiak was just on the other side of the peninsula, but the nearest town logistically was Anchorage.

We'd flown by bush plane from there, and it had taken quite a few flights to get us all in along with our provisions. It was these kind of logistics that made arctic digs so potentially expensive.

I'll never forget the first night there. We'd managed to set up all of our tents, which was necessary because of the hordes of mosquitoes, plus we were in bear country. Tents won't really protect you from bears, but you have a slight advantage when they can't see you. But the rest of our supplies were still stacked exactly as they'd been unloaded from the planes, waiting for us to organize them.

The old village sat on the edge of the beach, a large sunken area, indeed about to be washed away, just as the elder had told Dave. It had a rather ominous air about it, though I couldn't explain why.

After we'd all set up our tents, we scavenged driftwood from the beach and made a big fire, cooking dinner and sitting around the fire well into the late evening. Of course, it being summer in Alaska, it wasn't dark until midnight.

But the one thing I remember best about that evening was how subdued everyone was. There were about 15 of us, and even though we were tired, we had all been very talkative and excited until we actually arrived, then it seemed as if something had made us all pensive and quiet.

I remarked about it around the fire, and everyone agreed that the place felt rather spooky. I wondered if I hadn't predisposed the dig by mentioning what Dave had said about the spirits, but after it was all over, I talked to several other dig members and they all said they'd felt the same way from the moment they'd arrived.

That heavy ominous feeling pervaded everything the entire time, which ended up being much shorter than we had anticipated. We were prepared to spend the late summer and fall and had made arrangements for getting resupplied by bush plane, but we only stayed about three weeks.

I was worried when I ended the project that everyone would be upset and disappointed, but that wasn't the case at all. There was more of a feeling of jubilation that we were leaving, and I found out later that everyone was pleased with my decision. And I also found out that I wasn't the only one who had qualms with what we were finding and seeing.

But back to the dig. Typically, the first few days of a project like that are spent getting organized and laying out anchor points for mapping the site. So, the first morning there, I took my mug of coffee and wandered over to the sod house to look around. A couple of my graduate students went with me, and to say we were amazed by what we saw would be an understatement.

Because the tundra was melting and the village sinking, stuff that have been frozen and buried for hundreds of years was now coming to the surface. I could see that time was of the essence, as things that had been preserved were now beginning to rot, especially the posts of the sod house, which differentiated what looked to be small rooms.

We stood on the edge of the large sod structure, not venturing into the actual dig site, for we didn't want to alter anything or cause damage. Archaeology is by nature destructive, but it's a very methodological form of destruction, and we try to save as much as possible.

But standing there, looking at the old mostly buried sod building, I could clearly see why the elder wanted us to come. Everywhere we looked we could see artifacts melting out from the sod—ulus (cutting tools), pieces of kayaks, baskets, bundles, eating utensils, and, almost at my feet, what looked like a belt of caribou teeth.

We ended up with over 1,700 intact artifacts just from our three-week dig, all which went to the stabilization lab at my university where they were studied and photographed. I eventually returned it all to the Yupik tribe, as we had agreed to do, where they put the artifacts in their own museum. There, the villagers could come see them, the tools and remnants of their ancestral culture.

While standing there, we also saw something that gave us pause. Something was shining in the sun, and we soon determined that some of the wooden posts of the structure's walkways were literally encased in sharp points, the kind the Yupik ground from slate and used with arrows. As we excavated the site, we found over 500 of these points, the result of the village being attacked. It was a grim introduction to our project.

As an arctic archaeologist, I had seen these slate points before, but I knew something was different here, though it took me awhile to figure out what it was—the points were much larger than any I'd seen before, at least twice as big and much heavier. This was puzzling.

We walked back to the camp site, talking with excitement about what we'd seen. It looked to be a major find.

I'm a light sleeper, so I pitched my tent over on the edge of our campsite. We were camped on the same level as the village, back a ways from the sea and near some willow thickets.

Mosquitoes love willows, but it was the best we could do. We all had lots of mosquito netting, and we would build big fires in the evenings and the drifting smoke would help keep the insects away.

I was pretty tired, as we'd been organizing supplies and getting ready for the excavation all day. I knew I would sleep well, and my head had barely hit my pillow when I was sawing logs. I slept well until I had to get up and relieve myself. I figured it was around 3 a.m.

I stepped out of my tent and walked a few feet towards the willows when I heard a strange droning sound, way off in the distance. I paused and listened, but couldn't figure out what it possibly could be. It almost sounded like a huge swarm of mosquitoes, but I knew they could never be that loud, as it was far away. It wasn't an airplane, nor did it sound like anything mechanical.

To this day I have no idea what it was, but I suspect it was something going on in the Yupik village where the elder lived, which was about 10 miles distant. Whatever it was, I had a bad feeling about it, and it all seemed to tie in with the ominous mood of the old sod house.

I was soon back in my tent, where I could still hear the sound, but not as clearly. I finally drifted back to sleep and forgot the whole thing until someone else mentioned it at breakfast. It seems I wasn't the only one who had heard it. None of us had any idea what it could've been.

The north country has many mysteries, tales of people lost and never found, and the natives have a repertoire of myths like nothing I've ever heard before or since. It's such a vast wild region that it's easy to understand how the human mind creates tales to try to explain the unknown. I felt like we'd had a taste of the mystery with the strange sound and the weird feel of the entire area.

Now the dig got into full swing. Almost everyone there had been on previous excavations and understood their roles well, and we were soon making good progress.

This was also the same day that we got a visit from the same Yupik elder who had invited us to come excavate the village of his ancestors. His name was Warren, and he had his eight-year-old granddaughter with him and wanted to show her what we were doing. He was very proud of his heritage and wanted to share it with her, light an interest in the history of her people.

Warren pointed to a ulu we had just removed from the site, saying to his granddaughter, "Look, here's an uluaq just like your mother uses to cut the heads off the salmon. The handle is very clever—it's shaped like a seal, but if you look at it just right, you'll see the outline of a whale."

I was surprised, for none of us had noticed the whale. Warren continued, "This is how we Yupik view things—nothing is simple, and everything is always changing."

I immediately took a liking to Warren and decided to ask him what he thought of the large slate points embedded in the wooden timbers. I had removed one and now held it in my hand, asking him if he'd ever seen anything like it.

To my surprise, his demeanor instantly changed, and he asked, "Did you find this here?"

I told him it appeared there were hundreds of them throughout the site. I was surprised by his reaction. He quietly whispered to his granddaughter to stay put, and he walked with me far enough away that she couldn't hear.

"I made a big mistake," he said. "You do not belong here. I'd heard stories from others about seeing spirits here, but I had no idea that this was one of *those* villages. It explains the events of last night in our village. We were visited by the dark ones, the spirits. I didn't understand why they came, but now I do. If you continue, there will be bad things happen here, as well as in our village. I'm going to have to ask that you and your expedition crew leave immediately."

I was beyond shocked. "Last night? Bad spirits? But we can't leave. We've spent a fortune to come here, and these people have all dedicated time from their lives to help excavate the village. It was my understanding that you personally invited us here to help recover items that would help preserve your own peoples' culture. Why would you change your mind so quickly?"

Warren stood silent for a moment, then said, "I'm sorry. I was mistaken. This village no longer belongs to my people. Yupik against Yupik is bad, but this wasn't Yupik against Yupik, but much worse. The village was desecrated. I'd heard the stories and didn't believe them, but now I do. You must go or you will bring the evil ones back to reclaim what's now theirs. They may already be here."

I was speechless as I watched Warren quickly collect his grand-daughter and leave on his ATV. I had no idea what was going on, but I knew we had no choice but to either leave or to somehow convince Warren to change his mind, which at that point didn't seem possible.

I sighed. I was sure it wasn't the first time that archaeologists had been kicked out of a site, but there seemed to be no rhyme or reason behind Warren's actions. What had he meant by one of *those* villages? It was all just too strange. And had the events he'd mentioned from the previous night had something to do with the droning sound we'd heard?

I desperately felt like I needed to contact Dave, to see if he knew what might be going on. The problem was, there was no cell phone service between where we were and Anchorage. I had a satellite phone for emergencies, but it was very expensive to use. Dave probably had no more idea what was going on than I did.

It was then that I recalled what Dave had told me when he'd first contacted me. Hadn't he said few would come near the village, that it was haunted by evil spirits? Hadn't some even claimed to have been chased while on snowmachines in the area?

Of course Warren knew all this, he'd been the one who had told Dave, so why the concern now? Something had happened the previous night at his village, which along with seeing the large slate point, had made him change his mind. None of it really made sense. I would just have to go to the village and talk more with Warren. The problem was that I had no way to get there.

I called a meeting with my graduate students, all who were getting class credit from the dig, and explained to them what had gone on. They had a lot invested in this expedition, and some would have to delay their graduation another semester if we canceled. I would let them help me decide what to do. I would try to avoid telling everyone else until I absolutely had to.

The consensus was to carry on until Warren showed up again, assuming he did, then we could discuss it with him further. We just didn't have enough information to go on, and we had already committed to doing the dig.

It was an uncomfortable situation to be in, but in actuality Warren had extended the original invitation, and he hadn't given us much of a reason to cancel, in my opinion. If it truly wasn't one of his peoples' villages, who was to say we couldn't continue? We would just carry on until we heard further from him. I'd dealt with superstitious people before, it was often part and parcel of doing archaeology.

We built a nice fire that evening and sat around it, talking about other adventures we'd had, getting to know each other a little better. It was really enjoyable, and I recall feeling that we had a really great bunch of people. It helped ease the discomfort I had with the day's events, with Warren throwing a wet blanket on the excavation.

All went well for a week or so, and we settled in doing the work we knew best, digging and recording what we'd found, many beautiful examples of perfectly preserved Yupik items.

One significant find was a basket that still had green grass in it, grass that grew 400 years ago. It was finds like that which made our day, made us all enjoy what we were doing in spite of the discomforts of camping with Alaska's epic mosquitoes.

But one find, and I admit this disturbed me, was a large pile of the broken remnants of kayaks, their intricately carved sterns and wood frames shattered, some still covered with perfectly preserved waterproof seal skins, but all destroyed as if stepped on or hammered with something heavy.

Kayaks are one of the most important tools the Yupik have, for they are heavily dependent on the sea, and to come upon such a cache of destroyed boats was unlike anything I'd ever seen. A Yupik kayak is a work of art, finely calibrated to the size of the owner and thereby often destroyed when the owner dies, as it's so perfectly fitted that it's often unusable by anyone else.

Were the owners of the boats killed and the boats thus destroyed? Or had something or someone destroyed the boats first, knowing it would limit the Yupiks' ability to provision themselves for the harsh northern winter? And why would the kayaks be inside the sod structure? It was a mystery.

We'd been there for a couple of weeks when I once again had to get up during the night. I vowed to not drink as much in the evenings as I pushed my way back to the edge of the willows. After relieving myself, I turned to walk back to my tent and swore I caught a glimpse in the moonlight of a big dark shadow behind me at the far edge of the thicket.

I felt like a fool for not carrying bear spray. I had lectured everyone when we'd first arrived that bear spray was to be carried at all times, regardless, as we were in prime brown bear territory.

I quickly crawled back into my tent, making sure my bear spray was handy. I could now hear something big walking around, though it seemed like it had gone more towards the central part of camp. Probably a bear looking for food, but we had carefully cached everything in bear-proof cans. It would hopefully soon figure this out and go away.

The next thing I knew, it was morning and I was waking from what felt like a very deep sleep. I could hear people talking, and I quickly got dressed and walked to the campfire ring, where hot coffee was brewing and most of the camp was already eating breakfast.

There was talk of the bear that had visited camp during the night, and a number of people had heard it, but no one seemed to have actually seen it. But everyone was unsettled by it, and for most, it was their first experience with a bear visitor.

It all seemed innocuous enough until we got to the excavation site, only to find that something or someone had strewn our tools everywhere, as well as removing the small red flags we'd used to mark sections of the dig and the locations of artifacts. The entire site was a mess. We had paper and digital maps we'd created as we went along, but it would be hard to reconstruct everything. It was a big blow to our work.

Had Warren come back during the night and destroyed everything? After all, he'd told us to leave. But to me, he didn't seem like the type to do something like that. He was more likely to come back with members of his tribe and ask us to leave through a show of force than to secretly destroy our work.

A few thought it must have been the bear that visited camp

during the night, but someone else pointed out that a bear couldn't simply pull flags up, but would instead have to dig them up.

We regrouped around more coffee, and I decided it was time to tell everyone what Warren had said earlier. I admitted to them that I was at fault for not being upfront about it, but I hadn't wanted to upset anyone. It hadn't made much sense to me anyway, given how cryptic Warren had been. But what had happened during the night had me worried, and I wanted everyone to have a part in the decision of whether we should stay or go.

There was a good bit of discussion, and almost everyone admitted to having feelings of trepidation from the day we'd arrived without even knowing what Warren had said. But we were finding really good stuff, the kind of artifacts that had never been seen in such perfect condition, and no one was ready to leave yet.

In the end, it was decided that we should give it another week or two and see what transpired. In a sense, having the site messed with made everyone want to stay even more. The artifacts we were finding could prove significant, and this was our only chance to save them. We agreed to move our tents closer to one another instead of them being so scattered around, kind of like circling the wagons.

That very same night the dreams started, and I found out later that I wasn't the only one having them. They were so incredibly vivid that over the next few days I started having trouble differentiating them from reality, and they continued until we left.

One of my students later told me that I was looking so haggard they wondered if I'd started drinking, though they knew the only alcohol permitted at the site was beer. Others started asking me if I felt alright.

The truth was, I felt terrible, and each night made it worse. The dreams made me unable to sleep, and it all took its toll. I got to where I was afraid to go to bed.

The first dream seemed like the prologue to a story, a story that was continued in each consecutive dream, as if in a saga. In that first dream, I was like an eagle, high in the sky above the sod house that we were now excavating, except it was as it must have been when first built. I could see people going in and out of the big earthen structure, women tending children and cooking, men going off to hunt and fish, all the activities one would expect to see in a Yupik village of that time.

As the sun began to set, everyone went into the house and barred the door. The feeling was now one of great omen, and I woke in fear and couldn't get back to sleep. I thought I could again hear the droning noise in the distance, but it seemed much closer than the previous time.

The next day, I was able to actually identify where the entrance to the house was located, a fact verified once we started digging and found the door supports. I was as surprised as everyone else, and I confided in my students that I'd dreamed about it. We decided that I had somehow noticed something that had led me to the discovery and that it had taken the dream to bring it to my consciousness.

That night, I had yet another dream, but in this one, the house was being attacked by large dark figures, though they didn't manage to get inside. They eventually gave up and left, but my dream continued, for as soon as daylight came, I saw many of the men run to the nearby sea to collect their kayaks, bringing them to safety inside the house, then again barricading themselves inside.

I woke, somehow sensing that I knew the answer to the mystery of why the kayaks were inside the house. They had been taken there for safekeeping, and whoever had attacked the house had smashed them.

I was beginning to feel that I'd somehow entered a portal into the past through my dreams, and I was now beginning to have trouble waking from them. It would take me several hours before I could think clearly. I was beginning to feel a deep grogginess that would go on through part of the day.

In my dream the next night, the black figures were back, again trying to penetrate the house, and this time they had a large log that they used to smash through the heavy door. There were a great number of the black figures, all carrying what appeared to be spears with heavy slate tips, and as they entered the house, there was a great sound of terror and screaming, until finally, all was quiet.

I woke, sweating and disoriented, and I could still hear the screams, a sound I'll never forget. Finally, the screams abated and were replaced by the droning noise, but it was now much closer and almost sounded like it was coming from the sod house.

I lay still, somehow knowing that there were dark figures standing just outside my tent. I now knew where the large slate points had come from, points too heavy to be effectively used by humans, but just about the right size and weight for the large spears carried by these ominous creatures.

Another mystery had been solved, but at that point I really didn't want to know more. I was ready to leave. Warren had been right, we didn't belong there, and I was beginning to fear for my own mental health, as well as for the safety of the entire group.

I don't know how long I lay there in terror, but as dawn arrived I finally heard footsteps walk away from my tent. I was frozen in fear until I heard voices coming from the campfire ring and knew that others were now up and about.

Everyone had heard the droning sound, and there was talk of leaving, but as the day wore on, everyone wanted to stay a little longer, as we were finding such interesting stuff. The daylight seemed to dissipate everyone's fears.

That next day was when we found the first skeletons, some with broken skulls and many with large slate points in their ribcages. We found 12, three of which were children, and even though I knew it was a significant find, I felt sick, for these were the very people whose screams I'd heard the night before.

Or was it just a dream? It had to be—how could I possibly hear something that had happened 400 years previous? It was impossible. My ability to tell reality from a dream was becoming less and less acute.

We were now bound by provisions that acknowledged that the remains belonged to the descendants of these people, the Yupik, and were required to report our find to a Yupik representative. In this case it would be Warren, the tribal leader for this area. The only problem was that we had no way to contact him.

I stopped the digging, and we spent the rest of the day inventorying and carefully packaging the artifacts we would take back with us. I wanted to have everything ready for when we decided to leave.

Even though it was a quiet uneventful day, it was a time of great internal distress for me. I was torn, for my instincts said we needed to leave as soon as possible, but I wasn't sure whether or not I was falling prey to my own superstitions and strange dreams. In spite of all that was going on, I wanted to continue the dig. We could carry on and inform Warren of the find later.

After dinner, everyone seemed somewhat somber, which I figured was probably from finding the skeletons. It had been apparent from the start that the house had been attacked, but we had now confirmed that whoever did it had been brutal enough to kill children, something that I felt would make anyone reflective. I pondered the fact that it would probably be easier to kill the children of another species than those of your own.

It was soon time to go to bed, but I felt severe anxiety at the thought of crawling into my tent. I toyed with the idea of asking one of my male students if I could share theirs, but it seemed like an imposition, so I decided to just sit by the fire and keep it going as long as I could and curl up there. I got my sleeping bag and pillow, wrapped myself in mosquito netting, then settled in, listening to the night owls and the crackling of the burning wood.

As I lay there, I thought of another dig I had supervised, but this one in northwest Alaska. It was an enigma, and I still hadn't figured it out, nor had any of the other archaeologists who had studied it. No one had seen anything like it.

It was different in that it consisted of a number of houses similar to the one we were now excavating, but they were all connected by a web of tunnels. Archaeologists had discovered similar structures in that region before, but typically only a couple of houses connected by one or two tunnels. This was extensive compared to anything previously found.

But what made the find so strange was that the houses were gigantic compared to the previous finds, not just in square feet, but in the depth and height of the structures. It was as if they'd been built for people eight or 10 feet tall, and the tunnels were likewise larger to accommodate such.

I disentangled myself from my sleeping bag and the netting and got up and dragged more wood to the fire, leaning against a large log, thinking. As an archeologist, I not only studied the past, but I also studied the present in order to better understand the past. One thing that stood out in my mind right then and there was the number of legends I'd heard or read that described a large creature that looked exactly like the ones in my dream.

Could the more northern village with the large houses have belonged to these creatures that some called Sasquatch? Had they studied human culture enough to mimic it and create their own houses, as well as implements such as spears?

Were they responsible for the destruction I'd dreamed about, the slaughter of the villagers whose skeletons we'd found that very day? How many more were inside the house, buried by years of collapsing tundra? I recalled Warren's words, "Yupik against Yupik is bad, but this wasn't Yupik against Yupik, but much worse."

Suddenly, for the first time in my life, I wished I'd become anything but an archaeologist. I scooted closer to the fire, then tossed a couple of large logs into the fire ring, shivering in spite of how close I was to the flames.

And it was then that I wondered if I hadn't just seen something glint in the firelight, something over by the willows, something about the size of a slate spear point, but perhaps one actually lashed to a spear.

It appeared that everyone else was asleep, for I saw no lights in any of the tents. I settled back against my pillow again, pulling my sleeping bag clear up to my neck. The thought of sleep made me claustrophobic, panicky. I would stay awake all night.

But instead, I fell asleep, and yet another dream plagued me.

I was a small boy, a Yupik, and I knew my parents were terrified, that something really bad was happening, though I had no idea what. My mother held me close to her chest, while my father stood in front of us, holding a spear in defense.

All around, I could hear the clanking of something hard against wood while people screamed in terror. These people were my family, and I could tell exactly who was screaming—my grandmother, my uncle...

Now, something really bad had entered the passageway to our part of the house. My father was a very brave man, usually the first to spear the walrus, a very dangerous animal, and yet I could tell he was very afraid. Suddenly, he threw his spear with all his might, and I could hear a grunt as it struck deep, followed by the sound of something large falling onto the floor. But that was soon followed by a cry from my father, as he was himself struck, falling back on top of us.

Suddenly, a large dark face appeared in the doorway, and I knew my mother and I would soon die. The face was that of a giant creature whose eyes were filled with blood and anger, and it had long hair all over its face. It soon stepped over my father's body and lunged for me, and I could see its entire body was covered in long dark-brown hair.

I quickly woke from the nightmare, stifling a scream, the dream was so real. As I became fully awake, I realized it was another dream, and yet, was it? For I could still see that face, that giant hairy hominid face, looking at me through the shadows of the fire, not more than 10 feet away. It was one of the most malevolent things I'd ever seen, and I knew it intended to kill me, just as its ancestors had killed the small boy I'd been dreaming about.

I yelled at the top of my lungs as I jumped to my feet, quickly grabbing a long stick from the edge of the fire, its end ablaze, and waving it at the monster. The creature grunted just like in my dream, but instead of attacking, it was soon gone, leaving a horrible stench in its wake.

My yell had awakened everyone, and the camp was soon astir with people asking what had happened. I frantically threw more wood on the fire, directing others to do the same, and we soon had a big bonfire going, which we all stood around.

I wasn't sure what to tell everyone, as I was skeptical that anyone would believe me, yet I wanted everyone to be aware and alert.

I decided to say it was a huge brown bear, one that hadn't been afraid of the fire and had come in to attack, but that I'd thwarted it with a fire stick. I then requested that everyone stay by the fire until daylight, as the bear had seemed predatory and might drag someone from their tent if they went back to bed.

Everyone seemed eager to comply, so we basically spent the rest of the night hunched around the fire, nervously looking over our shoulders. A few went to sleep there, but most stayed awake.

Dawn came, and we made a big breakfast of pancakes and freeze-dried sausage, along with several pots of coffee. It was then that I announced my decision to close the dig. We would pack everything up and hopefully I could get several bush planes to come and take us away before dark. I had no intention of spending another night there. Everyone looked relieved.

I used my satellite phone to make several calls, and we were fortunate enough to find a bush-flight service who could fly in and take us out that same day. We were even able to get all the artifacts out, mostly because none of them were very large.

It took several planes to get us all out. I was on the last flight out, and I asked my pilot to circle the site one last time in the late-evening light. As he did, I felt a combination of horror and deep sadness for the inhabitants of the big sod house, but I also felt a deep sense of gratitude that my group hadn't met the same fate.

I knew then that I had misjudged the Yupik people, for what I had thought was superstition had been a reality that was terrifying beyond comprehension. I would call Warren when I got home and tell him what had happened. I knew he would understand.

As it turned out, Warren was the only one that I ever told the complete story to, though I did talk some with my graduate students, who assured me they had also been having strange dreams and hearing weird night sounds and were happy to leave.

Back at the university, they helped me stabilize and archive the artifacts we'd recovered, which helped them get full credit for the dig. I eventually sent all the artifacts back to Warren's village.

Like I mentioned earlier, that was my last arctic excavation. My next and subsequent digs have all been in Arizona. My heart is still in the arctic, and I miss the grandeur of Alaska, but when I crawl into my tent at night, I have little fear.

I know I can never go back to the north country, at least not to excavate. In fact, I have trouble going anywhere very far from civilization these days, though the desert seems safe.

Finally, let me say that as a trained and highly experienced archaeologist, I am well aware of the ethics involved with keeping an artifact in one's own private possession. It's simply not something an ethical scientist would do, but at a certain point, I decided it was a simple choice between being ethical or going insane, so I voted to keep the small figure carved from walrus-tusk that I found in the sod house. My will states that it be returned to the Yupik, but I hope I can heal psychologically and return it to them long before I die.

It's a masterful carving of one of the beasts, or Bigfoot as some call them, right down to the fierce strange eyes. It's the only thing I have to remind me that I wasn't insane, that I really saw what I saw on that wild beach along Bristol Bay in Alaska, the night my whole outlook on life changed, the night of my paradigm shift.

4

THE BOOM TRUCK

I met Jerry one sunny afternoon at a produce stand in the little town of Palisade, Colorado, at the base of the immense Grand Mesa, the setting for his story. I'd stopped to get some of the town's famous peaches and noted a bumper sticker on a pickup in front of the stand that bore the words, "Bigfoot: Wanted Dead or Alive."

Well, given that most of the people I know would rather see Bigfoot alive, if they see him at all, I was intrigued. When I asked, Jerry laughed and said it was his way of recruiting new team members, as well as getting people to talk about it, maybe thereby revealing where he might find one.

He then went on to say he was a serious Bigfoot hunter, his efforts mostly limited to Grand Mesa. When I asked him to tell me more, he invited me to go sit with him in the small town park there, where we ate peaches and he told the following story. —Rusty

I don't mean to make this into a psychological analysis, Rusty, but the one thing about realizing that Bigfoot really exists, I mean actually seeing one, is that it creates a wedge between you and all those who don't believe you. I think that might be the hardest thing there is about my sighting.

It's made me see that most people, even some in my own family who I love and trust, refuse to believe in anything that might be frightening. Denial is a deeply ingrained human trait, and it's just really hard for me to realize how close-minded many people can be.

I mean, people who have known you since you were a baby and have always believed you, now no longer do, and worse yet, you know that deep inside they think there might be something wrong with you. I think that might be even harder than knowing there's a large dangerous creature out there.

But anyway, be that as it may, it's just something you have to learn to live with, and I now understand why people who've seen Bigfoot are reluctant to tell others about it. They don't want to be ridiculed, and many also want to forget that it's out there, because it's so unsettling. It's like seeing something that really traumatized you, and you just don't want to talk about it, like war veterans don't want to talk about their experiences.

I've noticed in a lot of reports that people have to come to grips with their sighting before they can talk about it, and some never do, so they refuse to corroborate a friend's sighting or whatnot, pretty much leaving that other person hanging.

I used to be very careful who I told this story to. I tried to tell one of my friends at one point, and he just laughed at me. That really hurt, and I don't see him anymore, partly because he was fairly brutal about telling me I'm crazy.

He's an outdoorsman, like I am, and I know he doesn't want to believe it because it will make him uncomfortable out there. I guess I don't really blame him, but it did create a big distance between us.

I don't know, maybe I am crazy, but I definitely went through a change, which I don't think would've happened if I'd just been imagining it. But let me say that part of that change may not have necessarily been for the better. I now realize that I'm a very stubborn person, even vengeful, and now I don't care who I tell my story to. The more the better. I now have a mission, which is to prevent others from being harmed, even if they don't believe.

Before I begin, I want to tell you that I had no awareness of

Bigfoot before this all happened. I was totally unaware that it could even exist. Sure, I'd heard of Bigfoot, but to me it was just a myth, folklore or something people liked to hear about for the thrill, kind of like ghosts. I paid no attention to any of the stories. In school, I was probably the only one of my entire class who didn't see "The Legend of Boggy Creek." I had no interest in it at all.

I guess some people like that kind of thing, and I've heard it's because of the lack of adventure in their lives, but I've never been one to like scary stuff. I won't even go to a scary movie. I was a total nonbeliever, so much so that Bigfoot wasn't even on my radar. When this all happened, I couldn't even categorize it as possibly being Bigfoot, as that was so far out of my mind's reach of possibility.

Now, afterwards, I've read a lot about Bigfoot, and most of what I've read makes the creature look benign and even friendly. It seems that in the majority of encounters the creature is simply acting territorial and trying to scare people away, and even when there are close encounters, it's not aggressive.

You'll soon see that this was not the case with me. I may have just had the bad luck to interact with Bigfoot having a bad day, but in all honesty, I don't think they're harmless. If the ones I encountered had the ability to act as aggressive as they did, then I believe they *all* have that ability.

OK, let me start by saying that I have kind of an unusual profession, though not *that* unusual. I call myself an arborist, though I think a real arborist knows a lot more about trees than I do, as I didn't go to college in horticulture or anything.

Basically, I trim trees, treat them for diseases, and sometimes even cut them down. I'm that tall skinny guy you see at your neighbor's on the ladder trying to figure out how to cut limbs off without getting killed. It's not all that risky of a business if you pay attention, though I have had some close calls.

Actually, more often than not, I use ropes and a harness to climb, and I'm pretty good at it, which is undoubtedly what saved my life when I met up with Bigfoot. I had a small boom truck before all this happened, but sometimes it was easier to just climb the tree, and I was a good climber.

The day that started all this was pretty much like all the others. I had a full schedule, and I knew I would have to keep moving to get everything done. It was summer, my busy season, and I try to make as much money as I can then because it has to carry me through winter.

I live in the small town of Cedaredge, Colorado. If you don't know where that is, it's on the western side of the state. I can usually keep pretty busy, even though Cedaredge is a small town, because it has a lot of cherry and apple orchards.

Cedaredge sets on the lower flanks of the world's largest mesa, called, appropriately enough, Grand Mesa. Most of the mesa is thick forest with over 300 lakes—and lots more mosquitoes than lakes. The mesa is about 50 miles long with over 500 square miles, topping out at around 11,000 feet, most of which is roadless and untouched.

There are some hiking trails on the edges of the mesa, but about the only people who ever go into its interior are hunters and cattle-men, and they generally have to go on foot or horseback. There is a small town on top called Mesa, which is near the small ski area of Powderhorn.

Though I normally wouldn't travel that far, I got a call from the town of Mesa asking if I would trim the trees along the city streets. It would take several days, and the pay was pretty darn good, so I accepted. I decided to take my boom truck, and it had a bench seat big enough to sleep on, so I grabbed my sleeping bag and a few groceries and headed for Mesa, eager to get the job done and collect that nice check.

The highway between Cedaredge and Mesa winds up to the top of the Grand Mesa, crosses through the forests, then gradually drops back down onto the other flank of the mountain. It's a good highway and very scenic, though it doesn't see a lot of traffic.

Well, it was a sunny summer day, and I was really enjoying the drive, when I had to stop to relieve myself. I always drink a lot of coffee in the morning, but in this case, it was a bad move. If I hadn't stopped, this story wouldn't have happened, and my life would have been all the better for it.

I pulled off the main highway onto a little dirt road that quickly dead-ended in a small meadow, then got out. It was a really pretty place, tall grasses with white-barked aspen trees all around and a small brook that wound along the edge of the trees.

I turned around to get back into my truck, then decided to take a short break and have another cup of coffee. This place was just too nice, and I wanted to stay and enjoy it for a few minutes. It seemed so totally peaceful, far away from the hecticity of trying to make money.

I pulled out my thermos and leaned back against my truck, enjoying the blue sky and warm sun on my face. Man, I would love to live forever in a place like this. Nobody to bother you, nice and quiet —and, of course, that's when I heard the noise.

It sounded like a cow in distress back in the trees. It started out as a low bellowing noise, then got more high-pitched and ended almost in a whimper, if a cow can whimper. Whatever it was, it was pitiful and sounded like it needed help.

I hadn't seen many cattle on Grand Mesa, but since cattlemen run them in all the other national forests, I know they're up there in the summer. My first instinct was to get in my truck, go down to Mesa, and call the sheriff. They could contact the rancher and he could come up and rescue it. After all, it wasn't my responsibility, it was his cow.

I really wish I had done that. I beat myself up daily for taking the course of action that I did. It was probably the stupidest thing I've ever done in my entire life. If I hadn't left my truck I would still have it, and my life would've gone on as usual, nice and quiet and steady. As it is, it will never be the same again.

Instead of listening to my gut, I let my emotions take over and felt sorry for the cow. I decided to walk back into the trees and see exactly what was wrong. If I couldn't help it, which I probably couldn't, I would at least be able to better inform the sheriff as to what was happening.

I pushed my way into the aspens towards the bellowing, but it stopped. I paused, listening, and it soon started up again, so I headed towards it. It didn't sound like it was very far away, but just when I thought I was close, it stopped again.

I was beginning to think that maybe the cow knew I was there and was frightened, because now it was completely silent. I pushed my way through the trees to where I was pretty sure the sound had originated, and sure enough, I came to a small boggy area, but there were no signs of anything amiss.

Okay, I thought, maybe the cow had gotten caught in the bog and then freed itself, even though I saw no signs of a struggle. Or maybe it was a cow calling for her calf, and now that they were reunited, she'd stopped bellowing. I did notice that there were no cow tracks anywhere, not even cow pies, which are part and parcel of cattle.

I turned back in the direction of my truck, puzzled, but also happy to not find anything disastrous. I wouldn't have to call the sheriff after all. I would just head on down to Mesa and get busy trimming trees, which was where I should be in the first place.

Well, it was not to be. When I started walking in what I thought was the right direction, I found I was going deeper into the forest. I soon emerged from aspens into a stand of tall blue spruce.

I immediately turned around and walked back the direction I'd come, back to the small bog. I stood there for awhile, swearing that I'd come in from the same direction that led me to the spruce. I'm not that easily turned around, even in a forest, and I've always had a pretty good sense of direction. Blue spruce are one of my favorite trees, so I would've been sure to notice the dusky blue trees had I walked by them on my way in.

I again went the same direction, coming again to the same spruce. This was definitely not the way. There was no way I wouldn't have noticed these big trees. I had been in aspens the entire time.

Oh well, no need to worry, I'd just gotten a little turned around. I headed in a direction about 45 degrees from my first path, now staying in the aspens and expecting to see my truck at any time. But instead of emerging from the tree line, I found myself again deeper in the forest.

I backtracked again to the bog, thinking how strange it all was. I'd spent a lot of time hiking and fishing in Colorado's back country, including in forests just like this, and I'd never had any trouble at all orienting myself.

I examined the ground, hoping to see where I'd walked through the grasses under the trees, but couldn't make anything out. How could I possibly walk just a hundred or so feet into a forest and become totally lost?

Well, not to panic, because I had one advantage over most people —I knew how to climb trees. I would just climb the nearest tree until I could see out, then I would go straight back to my truck, no big deal.

The altitude was high enough that the aspen forest was fading into pine and spruce forest, trees not so easy to climb with their stiff branches and scratchy needles. I found a large aspen and shimmied up, grabbing branches and pulling myself up until I was high enough to see out.

It didn't matter which direction I looked, all I could see was thick forest. There was literally no sign of a road or highway or any kind of human activity. Come to think of it, I couldn't hear anything either, not the sound of even one vehicle. There's not a lot of traffic on that highway, but not to hear anything seemed odd.

I slipped down out of the tree, tore a strip from my red shirt and tied it around a branch, then once again started walking in the direction I was sure the highway had to be, paying close attention to the direction of the shadows of the trees so I would stay on course.

After what I estimated to be about a quarter of a mile, I hadn't found anything. I turned around and went directly back to my red flag, then once again, using the shadows of the trees as directional guides, I went the opposite way. After awhile, I had again found nothing.

I did this two more times, thereby knowing for sure that I had walked about a quarter of a mile in all four directions. I knew I was starting from the same place each time because of the red strip I had tied to the branch. I also knew that I hadn't walked anything like a quarter of a mile from the road, so I should have found it right away.

Of all the darndest things! I grew up in Colorado, had hiked probably hundreds of miles all told in the backcountry, and now I step off the road to check on a cow and get lost. I would never live this one down.

It was then that a bolt of fear went straight through me. Was I actually really lost? I'd never been lost in my entire life. How could I be lost?

For some reason, I remembered what they tell little kids to do when they get lost—sit down and stay put. So, I sat down under a big aspen tree, waiting for I don't know what, trying to collect my thoughts, because there was no one who would even notice I'd gone missing, since I lived alone.

But wait! I could tell the direction from those same tree shadows I'd been using. I knew what time it was, approximately 10 a.m., and it was summer, so the sun had to be pretty much due east of me, meaning the shadows would point toward the west. I had stepped off the eastern side of the highway, so if I went straight west, I would eventually intersect it.

I now had a plan. I felt very hopeful, knowing that if I paid attention and kept going west, I would eventually come to the road. So off I went, bushwhacking through the trees, hoping at any moment to catch sight of the highway.

It was hard work, so I stopped frequently to rest, and it was during one of those moments that I heard the sound of someone hitting something hard with a big log way off in the distance.

This was great! Maybe I would come upon a logging operation if I headed that direction, or maybe it was just someone cutting firewood, but in any case, it had to be another human, and they could help me find my truck.

I took off in the direction of the sound, even though it was the complete opposite of where I'd been going. I was so afraid that whoever it was would stop that I started running, dodging trees and underbrush as best I could.

I could now see ahead where the trees seemed to thin out, as if coming to a meadow, and I slowed to a walk, puffing and trying to catch my breath. Everything was beginning to look familiar again. Had I come to the road? How could I have possibly gotten so far away?

I was now at the edge of the trees, and sure enough, there sat my truck. Strangely, the sound seemed to be coming from it, as if someone were beating on it.

My intuition said to step back, and I did, hiding behind a tree. I could make out something over behind the truck bobbing up and down, and from the sound, I could tell that it was somebody hammering on my truck.

What the heck? Why would someone be hammering on my truck, especially out here in the middle of nowhere? I could understand maybe trying to break into it, but to just mindlessly hammer on it?

I was unarmed, and whoever it was obviously had a hammer or big stick, so I chose to stay hidden in the trees, not sure what to do. At least I wasn't lost anymore, though I was still puzzled at how totally disoriented I'd been.

Now this person was coming around the truck to where I could see him better, and I sure wasn't prepared for the shock. It wasn't a person at all! It was some kind of giant hairy man, and the more I could see of it, the less I wanted to see.

I can't describe how it made me feel, but let's just say it was a combination of shock, horror, disgust, and disbelief. It was truly one of the ugliest things I'd ever seen, especially with its long dark hair hanging down from its body.

My shock quickly turned into the deepest most visceral fear I've ever known. I had to hide, and quickly. I knew from the horrible look on its face that I would be the next to receive the hammer treatment, though it was actually using a thick log. I could now see where the whole driver's side of my truck had been smashed in to the point that I knew I wouldn't be able to open the door.

The truck looked like it would still be operable if I could somehow get to the passenger door and slip inside, but doing so without this thing seeing me seemed totally impossible.

At this point, I had no desire to go back into the forest after having gotten so thoroughly disoriented. The last thing I wanted was to be lost again, especially with this thing around. I somehow needed to stay put, but hidden, until it left.

Now the creature paused from its destruction, looking straight in my direction. I knew it couldn't see me through the thick brush I was behind, but did it have some sixth sense telling it I was here? More likely, it could smell me.

I knew I didn't have a chance against this thing. It was huge and apelike, very agile looking, whereas I was a mere human, pretty much at the mercy of whatever defensive measures my brain could come up with, a puny brain that wasn't cooperating at the moment.

I felt hopeless, helpless, and totally vulnerable as the creature started walking towards me. The closer it came, the more I could see how truly huge and muscular it was. It reminded me of a cross between a gorilla and a walrus, heavy and massive, yet looking as if it would be able to run with incredible agility and speed. I knew it would be fast, just from the size of the muscles in its legs.

I tried to quietly slip away, but I soon panicked and ran. The beast let out a bellow, and it was then that I knew what I had heard earlier over by the bog was no cow, but was one of these things. The sound made the hair stand up on the back of my neck.

Grand Mesa is capped with a thick layer of basaltic lava, with outcroppings forming small cliff bands here and there, one of which ran right behind where I'd been standing. I managed to scramble up to the top of the outcropping, but I knew that my attempt to escape would soon be overshadowed by the agility of the creature.

I stood, preparing to die, when it occurred to me that I had one advantage—my weight. This creature must weigh a good 500 pounds or more, and I weighed about 160. I couldn't outrun it, as I knew it was too fast, but I could maybe, just maybe, climb into a place that its weight would keep it from going, a place exactly like the tall slender aspen that grew next to the rock outcropping.

I was sure the creature could climb much better than I could, but was it smart enough to not climb a tree that couldn't hold its weight? I swung myself over to where the tree touched against the rocks and found a foothold, then started climbing.

I was used to having a rope and climbing harness, and I was nervous that I would fall, but I tried to concentrate on what I was doing instead, and I was soon about 25 feet up. Would the tree hold me? Aspens aren't well-known for having large branches, so it was hard to find footholds, and the higher I went, the more slender the trunk got and the more it swayed, but I continued to climb. I had no choice, as it was my only hope.

I guessed the tree to be about 40-feet tall, an old-timer in the world of aspen trees, a species not known for its thickness, even at tall heights. I pulled myself up as far as I could, now maybe at 30 feet.

The tree was swaying so much I thought it would break, but I held on and remained as still as possible, hoping the beast wouldn't see where I'd gone, as the rock outcropping and steep slope hid me. Once it topped the rocks, though, I knew I would be in trouble if it looked up. I tried to pull the branches around me, but I knew I wasn't hidden.

I smelled the thing before I saw its head bob up as it came out on top of the rocks. By then, the tree had stopped swaying, and I held my breath in terror, for now I could see up close what I was up against. The smell made me want to gag, and it was all I could do to not cough from the sulphuric gassy odor—one cough would seal my fate.

It was close now, and I could see the sheer size of this monster. I felt like a complete idiot. The thing could easily snap this aspen tree in two, bringing me down and probably killing me, or even shake me out of the branches. My only hope was that it wouldn't realize where I was. I held my breath and tried to be as still as possible.

The beast topped out on the outcropping and looked around, seeming puzzled. Its huge deep-set eyes stared off into the distance, searching to see where I'd gone. I then saw it raise its head as if smelling the air, though I guessed that its sense of smell wasn't as good as I might have thought, as its nose was flat against its face. Animals with a good sense of smell typically have snouts, like dogs or bears.

Still holding my breath, I was surprised to see the creature take off, following my path back through the woods, seemingly oblivious to my being up in the tree. Perhaps it was scenting the way I'd come, and good luck with that, for I'd been tramping all over that darn forest. It must've had a somewhat good sense of smell, though, to follow my trail like that.

I knew time was of the essence, and I quickly slipped down from the tree and ran as fast as I could to my truck. I was able to slip into the passenger side, then over into the driver's seat and start it up, which surprised me, for I had no idea how bad the damage was.

As I began turning around, I noticed that one of my back tires seemed to be going flat, but I didn't slow down. Just then, I looked in my rear-view mirror to see a big black face. The monster was behind me! I gunned it, but suddenly it was in front of me! No, wait, this was a different one, a second one!

I kept going faster and faster, the tire thump-thumping along, and I knew I was probably going to eventually come to a standstill once the tire was down to the rim. I'd be totally dead in the water with these two monsters after me. My only hope was to get out to the main highway before that happened.

I was going pretty darn fast for the dirt road I was on, at least 45 m.p.h., when I started seeing red. Now, I should tell you I'm part Irish, though I don't know if that really had anything to do with it, but I'm a pretty mild guy until I'm pushed over the edge. But at that point, I tend to have a pretty darn hot temper.

There was something about having these two beasts chasing me that just didn't seem right. I hadn't done a darn thing to them, and I was now suspecting them of luring me into the forest with their fake cow in distress sound.

It occurred to me that the only reason I hadn't been attacked by them sooner was because I managed to get myself lost and not return the direction they thought I would. I think this threw them off, and they instead decided to destroy my truck—or maybe they thought the hammering would bring me back to it, which it had.

I'd worked for years to buy that boom truck, and I was pretty sure my insurance company wouldn't cover something like Bigfoot damage. I was thinking all this kind of wryly as I was gunning my truck, also wondering how many minutes of life I had left if I destroyed my rim and axle.

I don't know how my mind held so many thoughts at once, but I do recall the predominate feeling I had was one of burning anger. I'd gone from horror and extreme fear to an uncontrollable rage. I suddenly wasn't afraid anymore, because I was going to take these creatures out with me.

Just then, I turned my wheel enough that I hit the Bigfoot running along near my front fender, tossing its body into the air in what seemed like slow motion. The second Bigfoot gave up the chase, stopping to help the first one. I wanted really badly to turn around and go after the other one, but by now the tire was so flat it was difficult to steer. Besides, I was almost back to the highway.

I was soon back on the highway, bumping along. I knew I had to get as far away from the side road as I possibly could before my truck conked out. Hopefully someone would come along soon and help me.

I kept looking in my rear-view mirror, but saw nothing. I knew I'd hit the first Bigfoot pretty hard, and even though it was large, I'd felt like I'd done it a good deal of damage. A later examination of the fender on that side of my truck showed a big dent where I'd hit it.

Well, I think I'd gone maybe a half-mile at the most when the tire wore down to the rim, halting any forward progress. I was dead in the water. This was unacceptable to me, for I was still well within range of the Bigfoot. There was literally nothing stopping it from coming after me and finishing the job, but there was also nothing I could do.

I sat in the truck, shaking from anger and fear. All I could do was pray that someone would come along, and I continued to look in my rear-view mirror for a black figure. There was no cell service on top of the mesa, at least not where I was, so I was unable to call for help.

It seemed like I sat there forever, but it was probably less than 15 minutes when I could see a car coming down the highway. I jumped out and frantically flagged it down, worried that the driver would think I was some kind of lunatic.

It was an older retired fellow out for a scenic drive, and he took me back to my home in Cedaredge. To make a long story short, I hired a tow truck, and we went and got my boom truck. It cost me a fortune to get it back home. There was no point in taking it to a body shop, for the damage was too extensive.

I did manage to get my insurance company to pay for it, which helped a great deal, and they totaled it out. I told them I'd left the truck to go for a short hike and someone had vandalized it while I was gone, which was all true, though with a few pertinent facts omitted.

I didn't buy another boom truck, but instead took the money and put it into savings. I decided to cut back on the tree trimming and just work part-time.

The rest of my time is now spent Bigfoot hunting. I know that sounds crazy, but I no longer have any fear of them, and I've managed to get a few of my buddies interested. We go out well-armed, and we're all just crazy enough that if we ever do find a Bigfoot, it'll be history before it knows what hit it.

I'm hoping we can be the first to actually bring in a body, and I have absolutely no qualms about this. After seeing how brutal and ruthless these creatures can be, I wouldn't feel bad if they were all exterminated. I'm 100% convinced that many of the missing people in America's forests have had run-ins with Bigfoot. These are not gentle creatures just wanting to be left alone. I know that saying this will anger many Bigfoot fans, but I believe it's true.

I can still see that big ugly face looking at me, and I remember the deep fear it instilled in me when it started coming after me. If I hadn't been able to climb that tree, there is no question that I would now be one of the missing. And I now carry a GPS so I'll never get lost again.

If me and my buddies can save even one other innocent human from such a horrible fate, all our time will be well spent. Some people think I'm crazy, but let's just hope they're never in the situation I was in up on that mesa—but if they are, I hope they can climb trees.

5

THE NOTOM HOUSE

I received an email from Diana one gray winter's day when at home, wishing I had something interesting to do. I sometimes work myself into a frazzle during fly-fishing season, and it's hard to slow down when winter comes.

Diana said she'd read some of my books and would like to share her story with me if I was interested. Of course I was, and we were soon talking on the phone like old friends. The following is the story she told. —Rusty

Rusty, I guess I should start by telling you about my friend, Hannah. We went to school together and were roommates in college. She was an art major, and I majored in psychology, and though we were pretty different, we were still good friends. This was at the University of Utah in Salt Lake City.

Hannah is important to this story in that I would've never gone down to the desert except for her. After we graduated, she ended up getting her real-estate license, though she still did her art on the side. I kind of lost track of her for awhile, but then I found out she was living in the tiny desert town of Hanksville, Utah.

Hannah was now Hanksville's only real-estate agent, and I think she'd maybe sold one house in the tiny town. But she didn't care, as it gave her plenty of time to paint landscapes and help her husband run the motel they'd bought there.

Hanksville is on the way from points north to Lake Powell and Capitol Reef National Park. It gets lots of tourists, though most of them stop only for food and gas, as there's not much else to stop for.

I've since married and have kids, but at the time I was single, working for a child protection agency in Salt Lake City as a counselor. It was a very stressful job, for I was seeing the seedier side of humanity. Some of the cases I dealt with were heartbreaking, and I was beginning to question my ability to continue in the profession. I was feeling like I'd screwed up royally in my career choice.

I needed a break, time to reanalyze the direction my life was going. I had a few weeks of vacation time coming, so I decided to take off, though I had no idea where to go. All I knew is that I wanted to get as far away from people as possible.

Well, Hannah said that if I came down to the desert, I could get away and restore my sanity, and she knew just the place for that.

In retrospect, it's almost comical. I was going to this place to regain my balance, to figure out what I wanted to do with the rest of my life, and yet it ended up traumatizing me more than my job ever had.

Between Hanksville and Capitol Reef National Park is an area called Notom. It's not really a town, just a loose community of a few ranches and, more recently, a few second homes for people who want to get away—I mean, *really* get away, because Notom is miles from the nearest town. I read that it was settled in 1883 and had only 20-some families at its height, and was now the jumping-off place for exploring Capitol Reef's eastern edge.

Even though there's really nothing much there, it's a beautiful setting with the Henry Mountains in one direction and the big white sandstone domes of the national park in the other. It's truly one of the most unique places one could ever live, and because it's surrounded by public lands, it will never be developed.

Hannah told me she had a real-estate listing in Notom, a fantastic house that she was sure the owner would be interested in renting out for a short period. She'd had the listing for over six months and there hadn't been one showing, and she was doubtful it would sell soon, if at all.

Not many people wanted to live in such a remote area with the nearest neighbor a good half-mile away and the nearest town almost an hour's drive, a small town with little there when you did arrive. And since it was the heat of summer, the tourists wouldn't be as numerous.

She emailed me the listing, which had photos of the house and which she called a "Hidden Treasure," and I was pretty much speechless.

A lot of people come to the desert and build homes with a Southwest look, usually Pueblo architecture with stucco exteriors, but this house looked like it came straight from some upscale architect's desk in New York or Chicago.

The house was very urban looking with its huge walls of glass and steel beams, and with burnished-red concrete patios all the way around the exterior. It had a second story retreat that consisted of a huge master bedroom and large double glass doors that opened onto a deck.

The photos showed an interior with lots of stainless steel and tile, floor to ceiling windows, and stamped concrete floors that matched the exterior patios. The furniture was modernistic, a sleek no-nonsense Danish look, and it had a kitchen that looked like it was from a gourmet cooking magazine.

And that was just the beginning. All that glass looked out upon a stunning landscape of mountains in one direction and the national park in the other. And with no neighbors, one could just walk out the door and go in any direction they chose for their daily hike, including down the hill to aptly-named Pleasant Creek, a riparian wonderland of willows and huge old Fremont cottonwoods.

I sighed. Ah, to be rich. I would buy that house in a second, and I was surprised that the asking price was only $495,000. Don't get me wrong, that's still a lot of money in my book, but if that house were in a place like Salt Lake City, it would cost a million dollars or more. Of course, if it were in the city, it wouldn't be the same.

Hannah called me not long after to tell me I was in. The owners had agreed that I could rent the house for three weeks, and my black Lab, Mambo, was also welcome.

Before you ask, and everyone always does, Mambo stands for Mamma's Boy. Mambo was originally called Max, but he's so attached to my hip that everyone called him Mamma's Boy—Mambo for short.

I asked Hannah why the owners were selling such a unique place, and she said it was a couple from Seattle who had fallen in love with the desert but weren't able to visit enough to justify the expense. She thought that they'd also become disenchanted because they were older and had underestimated their desire to be around amenities.

Wow, was I excited. This looked to be exactly what the doctor ordered. Three weeks in a quiet pristine place with no one to bother me, just me and Mambo.

I would stock up on groceries, get lots of teas and biscotti and things like that so I could sit around and be indolent and treat myself like royalty, soaking in the big Jacuzzi tub while reading mystery novels.

Keep in mind that I lived in a small townhouse in the heart of the city with only a small yard for Mambo, and you can imagine my excitement at being in such a place.

On my way, I stopped in Hanksville and had lunch with Hannah, getting the key and directions to the house. She wasn't able to visit long, but promised to come see me at the house in a week or two. We could catch up then on what we'd been up to.

I drove on down the blue highway from Hanksville to Capitol Reef, turning off on the Notom Road right at the entrance to the park. The Notom Road wasn't paved, but it looked like it was well maintained, and it wasn't long until I turned off onto a side road, crossed a bridge over Pleasant Creek, and drove up a long hill to the house.

It was everything I'd hoped for and more. I let Mambo out and he ran around, excitedly sniffing at everything and generally being a real live-wire as I unloaded my stuff. He seemed as impressed with the place as I was.

We walked around to the back of the house where a large outdoors rock fireplace was surrounded by a half-dozen patio chairs. A neat pile of firewood was stacked nearby, and I decided to have my dinner out there that very evening, enjoying the stars and quiet. I would have barbecued corn on the cob with fire-roasted potatoes and hamburgers.

I wandered around the house for a bit, getting settled in, feeling like someone very special. How many people could stay in a house like this in a setting so gorgeous? Right now, only one—and that was me, at least for a few weeks.

The house had central air conditioning and was nice and cool, and I kicked back in a leather recliner in the living room, drinking lemonade and gazing out at the Waterpocket Fold, a long sandstone reef that stretched for miles and defined the edge of the park. None of the house had curtains—no need for them out in the middle of nowhere, so being inside was almost like being outside.

I was glad I'd brought my camera, for this would be a perfect place to try my hand at taking some night photos, something I'd recently become interested in.

I can't describe how this all affected me—I could feel the tension in my neck and shoulders fading, replaced by a feeling of peace and solitude. Maybe I should become an artist like Hannah, I mused, and live in the desert. The only problem was how to support myself.

That evening, after it had cooled off, I built a fire in the flagstone fireplace, and Mambo and I had a delicious dinner. After we'd eaten our fill, he seemed as content as I was to just sit and watch the stars come out as the sun gradually set, fading into the far west.

I felt like we'd both died and gone to heaven. And though we had three weeks there, I already began wondering how we'd be able to leave and go back to the city.

Well, I found out that I needn't have worried about that, because when the time came, we were more than happy to go.

After awhile, the sound of a pack of coyotes calling in the distance reminded me that we should go inside and go to bed, as I was so tired I'd been nodding off there in the lounger.

We climbed the spiral staircase upstairs to the master bedroom, where I crawled into bed and turned out the lights, amazed that I could lie there and see the starry sky and distant horizon almost as well as if I'd been outside.

It had been a long day with packing and the drive down from Salt Lake, then getting settled in. I expected to sleep like a baby, but I found instead that I felt restless and had a feeling of what I can only describe as ennui.

I finally drifted off, dreaming I was in a huge desert, windblown with no shelter, watching as the wind drifted sand all around me, sure I would soon be completely buried and die.

It was the weirdest dream I'd ever had, and when I woke the next morning, I could understand why, for a fierce wind had come in from the west, blowing dirt and sand in huge sheets that looked like waves in a wild and dangerous ocean. I could even hear larger bits of sand hit the big windows of the house like a sandblaster.

I took Mambo out for a brief moment, but he wanted right back inside after watering a nearby rock. I'd never seen such winds, but by afternoon they'd subsided, replaced by huge black clouds that pushed in and soon covered the distant mountains in an ominous shroud.

It was soon pouring, a real gully washer, and I can tell you that being in basically what felt like a glass house and watching a huge thunderstorm was quite an experience. It was like being outside yet with none of the danger, something I'll never forget, with lightning popping all around and thunder shaking the glass panes.

Before long, I could again hear what sounded like the wind, yet it was different. The rain had now moved on up the valley, and I stepped outside with Mambo, curious to know what this new sound was.

I walked to the edge of the hill, then took Mambo back inside, not wanting him to inadvertently run down the hillside to where I could now see a muddy froth boiling up from the banks of Pleasant Creek.

It was a flash flood. The house sat high enough above the creek that there was no danger, and I decided I would walk down as far as was prudent and take photos. After all, it was something one didn't see every day, though I knew it wasn't unusual in the desert where everything was sandstone and the water had nowhere to go but to course down the creeks and gullies.

I left Mambo inside and carefully made my way down the hillside until I was afraid to go any farther, for the water appeared to still be rising. I stood on a rock and watched as the small stream filled with froth and logs and who knew what.

It was pretty exciting, and I managed to get some really good photos, as well as a short video of what appeared to be a dark-brown cow floating down in the muddy water. I have to admit I wasn't too crazy about that part.

It again started to sprinkle, so I climbed back up to the house. Mambo had never been so happy to see me, which I found odd, but I figured it was from the lightning and thunder. I made a cup of hot tea and gave him a biscuit and settled down in the big recliner to look at my photos.

It was amazing, especially the video, which to be honest was kind of scary. And there went that poor cow, floating on by in the froth.

Or was it really a cow? I paused the video and took another look. Something wasn't quite right. I examined several stills, trying to get a closer look. The object was large, like a cow, and it had dark hair, like a cow, but the shape was off.

The more I studied it, the more it looked like a bear, and yet it wasn't a bear either. What the heck was it? An ape, was what I wanted to say, but that made absolutely no sense at all. It was too big, and there were no apes in North America, especially in the Utah desert. And it had long flowing hair.

I kept looking at the video over and over, trying to make sense of it, but with no luck. I finally went back outside and again walked down to where I could see the creek. The water had dropped considerably just in the short time I'd been inside.

It was the start of the monsoon season in the desert, when wet storms would come up from the Baja region, bringing most of the annual precipitation and cooling everything off. It looked like it had blown over, so I decided to take Mambo for a walk. We would walk the opposite direction of the creek, over to the desert between the house and the main road.

Everything had been thoroughly soaked, but since it was sandy, it wasn't muddy. We walked over to some large junipers, where I noticed Mambo was interested in something. I went to see what it was, only to find to my distaste that it was a dead animal, or what was left of one.

I knew this was part and parcel of rural living, but I wasn't real happy about finding something like this so near the house. I would have to watch Mambo and keep him out of it, for I don't think there's a dog alive that doesn't like to roll in bad stuff.

I really didn't want to look at it, as I found it distasteful, but I did want to know what it was. It was too small to be a deer and kind of looked like a coyote, but kind of not, as it was bigger. About all that was left was the hide, which had the coloration and spots of what looked to be some kind of domestic dog, though the hair didn't look right.

I wondered what had happened to it. Obviously its owners had never found it, for if they'd known about it, surely they would've buried it. Had it belonged to the couple that owned the house?

What I found next was kind of odd, but I didn't think that much about it at the time, as I had no frame of reference. Near the dead animal, deep in the sand, were several large tracks that were much bigger then my own footprint, as well as much deeper.

I assumed it was a man, someone heavyset, but I was puzzled as to why they would be running around barefoot. Had they seen the dog? If so, why just leave it there?

I knew I might be overreacting, but I now had a nagging feeling that I should keep a close eye on Mambo and not let him run off-leash, which took part of the fun from being out there in the sticks.

Oh well, I thought, a responsible dog owner really shouldn't let their dog run, no matter where they were. But wasn't running free part of being a happy dog, at least where they can't get into any harm?

I went back to the house, feeling kind of deflated between seeing the dead animal in the creek and the dead animal under the juniper. Why did nature have to be so harsh?

It was now evening, and I made a dinner of tuna sandwiches, feeling a bit too desolate to want to cook. All I really wanted to do was go sit in that big Jacuzzi tub and get lost in a book. I was feeling kind of depressed, probably because of all I'd seen, including the raging flash flood. Things weren't as benign here as I'd hoped for.

I wasn't sure where the house got its water, though I suspected a well. In any case, I didn't want to be a big water hog, but I sure enjoyed soaking in that tub. This seemed to really relax me and make me forget everything, and I soaked until I was about to wrinkle into a prune.

I got into my pajamas, again amazed at the view of the night sky visible from the bedroom. But I was restless, and I got up and went downstairs for awhile, then went back to bed. As I crawled in, I saw a button by the nightstand, and though I didn't know what it was for, I pushed it.

Low and behold, the bedroom had mechanized shades! By holding down the switch, I could make the shades go down, covering the huge windows. I suddenly felt a sense of protection and security, realizing that my restlessness had been from feeling somewhat vulnerable. That night, I slept well.

The next day, I decided to take Mambo and walk him down the road a ways. It was about a mile to where the side road to the house met the main Notom Road. There, a bridge crossed Pleasant Creek. I would walk down and see if any damage had been done by the flash flood.

When I got there, I could see where a backhoe had dug mud from around the bridge. It looked like the creek had almost washed the bridge out.

As I stood surveying the damage, a man came by on a horse. He had silver hair and a lined suntanned face, and I figured he was one of the local ranchers, which it turned out he was, introducing himself as Will. He told me that a cow had come down and blocked the water from flowing under the bridge, and indeed the bridge had almost been washed out.

I asked him what they had done with the cow, and he gave me a strange look, saying it had finally washed on down the creek. For some reason, I felt that he wasn't telling me the whole story.

I knew it was odd to ask about the cow, but I still wasn't convinced that was what it was, and I thought he might have something to say about that. Instead, he asked if I was renting the house or had bought it.

I told him I would only be there a few weeks, and he told me that the previous owners hadn't been back for over a year, and everyone was wondering if the house would ever be inhabited again.

He actually used those words, *inhabited again*, which struck me as really odd. Why wouldn't the house be inhabited again? It was a perfectly good house, in fact, it was an outstanding house, it was just a matter of finding the right person for it.

I decided it might be a good thing to tell Will about the dead dog, as he might know who it belonged to. He said he didn't know anyone who had lost a dog, but would I mind showing him where it was?

I didn't mind at all, hoping maybe he could identify it, so we headed back up the road, me and Mambo walking alongside Will on his sorrel horse who he said was named Tommy. He told me about his Mormon ancestors who'd helped settle Notom, and how things were changing here, and not necessarily for the best, with so many tourists coming in.

We finally came to the juniper stand, and I showed him the dead dog. Will got off Tommy and spread out the hide.

"This isn't a dog at all, my dear," he said somberly. "It's one of my missing calves. And I'm not liking the looks of these footprints next to it. They look like they've been here awhile, but I think it's time I told you to be really careful out here, as all is not what it seems right now."

I felt a deep sense of trepidation. "What do you mean?" I asked.

"I don't want to unnecessarily alarm you," Will replied. "But just be careful. Don't go out at night, and if I were you, I would go back to your own home."

With that, Will got onto Tommy, touched his hat and said goodbye.

I slowly walked back to the house with Mambo, wondering what it all meant. Don't go out at night? Why not? Were there mountain lions around? Is that what had killed the calf? But why had he remarked about the footprints, and what did he mean when he wondered if the house would ever be inhabited again?

Wow. This was supposed to be a time of relaxation and reprieve, but I was beginning to feel like someone who'd been thrown into a mystery novel.

I stretched out in the recliner with a hot cup of tea, watching the colors in the clouds as the sun started to go down, thinking about everything that had happened. I'd heard that people in rural areas typically weren't fond of outsiders. Was Will purposely trying to get me to leave? Did he resent having a city girl like me staying in his family's historic territory? After all, he had mentioned how things were changing and not necessarily for the best, with so many tourists coming in.

It just didn't make sense. He didn't seem like that kind of guy at all. If anything, he'd been open and friendly, at least until he saw the calf, then he seemed worried and had given me fair warning, though I had no idea about what.

As a trained psychologist and someone who worked closely with people, I'd developed a keen sense of intuition and an ability to read between the lines. I felt that Will was being honest, but I also felt that he was hiding something significant. Of course, he'd as much as said he was, but I felt that it was something beyond the norm.

Back home, before I'd gone to Notom, I'd done some internet research on the area. There wasn't much available other than some information on the geology and prehistory, but I had found a forum of backcountry hikers who shared information about good areas to camp and hike. There was a posting by a woman who'd been a leader at an outdoor school where she told about bringing students to camp nearby.

There were about 20 of them, 17 high-school students and three leaders, and they had so many strange incidents that the school never brought a group back to the area again. It seems that they'd been stalked in the dark, heard weird noises, and seen glowing eyes, among other things.

The comments she received in response basically told her that what they'd seen were some of the herd of buffalo that range in the nearby Henry Mountains, nothing supernatural or strange. She'd replied that there was no way it was buffalo, then had left the forum in anger.

I had found it rather strange that, especially if it were buffalo, she would get so angry. She must've truly thought it was something inexplicable to be so emotionally invested. Of course, you can't believe everything you read, especially on the internet, but the whole exchange left me feeling like they had indeed seen something, or at least thought they did. Her descriptions hadn't sounded like buffalo to me, and she'd become angry at everyone's refusal to believe there might be something unusual out there.

I had thought no more about it until that night, stretched out in the recliner, watching the sunset. Notom sat right smack in the middle of a vast wilderness, miles and miles of untouched land, and who knew what was really out there? I recalled reading that the Henry Mountains had been the last explored mountain range in the contiguous U.S.

Of course, the land now wasn't all that untouched, as it had been explored and used by cattlemen, miners, hikers, and other outdoors enthusiasts, but it was still basically uninhabited.

And there we sat, me and Mambo, prime targets for about anything out there, completely unarmed, with only glass walls for protection, and no mechanized curtains downstairs to hide us. We were sitting ducks.

I knew if I kept thinking about it, I could get myself pretty worked up, probably over nothing. So, instead, I went and made a nice dinner of pasta salad with homemade rolls and a nice tomato-bisque soup. I actually really enjoyed cooking, even though sometimes it seemed a waste since I was the only one around to enjoy it, though Mambo was always game to try anything I made.

Now the house seemed warm and cozy, and I soon forgot about Will and all the strangeness. It looked like a brilliant starry night, so I decided to step outside and see if I could get some good night shots.

Remembering what Will had said about not going out at night, I decided to set up my camera on the deck outside the master bedroom upstairs. I would be safe up there and would still have a great view of the night sky. It was as if whoever had designed the house had wanted to create a safe place for after dark.

It was pitch black and the stars hung in the sky like diamond dust. I'd never seen anything like it—it was breathtaking. The Milky Way hung across the sky like a giant silver belt of shimmering lights, and Sagittarius, which is near the galactic center of our galaxy where the stars are thickest, rose as high in the sky as it would get for the season. July was the prime time of the year for night-sky photos, and I was in the perfect place.

I set up my tripod out on the deck and fiddled with my camera as Mambo lay quietly at my feet. I was sure he was wondering what I was doing, as I didn't get to try my night photography skills very often.

I set my timer to 20 seconds, then waited, enjoying the stunning sight above me. Suddenly, Mambo jerked his head up, making the deck shake a little, and I knew the shot was ruined.

I reset my timer, again hoping to get a good photo. After it took, I looked at the LCD display and gasped—the camera's sensor always captures more than the eye can see, and the photo was incredible.

But now Mambo was trying to get back into the house, scratching on the patio door. This wasn't like him, as he always wanted to be right where I was, but I let him back in, noticing that he was shaking.

It was then that I saw something standing not far from the house. It was visible only because it was darker than the sand and looked like a black blob against it.

I thought of the outdoors forum and what they'd said about there being a wild buffalo herd in the Henry Mountains. Did they come down this low? It was probably on its way to Pleasant Creek for a drink.

I turned my camera in its direction, trying to focus on it, but it was too dark. I went ahead and took several photos anyway, hoping maybe one would turn out and I could see what it was.

But suddenly from nowhere, I panicked. Hadn't Will said to stay inside after dark, that it was dangerous? Had he been referring to the possibility that buffalo might be around? Buffalo are one of the most dangerous animals on Earth when they get angry. They're extremely fast and can pivot quickly on their front legs and gore you to death. But why would he be so secretive, if it was just a buffalo?

I calmed myself down. There was no way a buffalo could get up here. Mambo had to be afraid because he'd never seen one and yet instinctively knew it was dangerous.

Mambo was again scratching on the patio door, I assumed wanting back out, so I reached over and opened it. He stood there, whining, refusing to come out, and I knew he was worried about me and wanted me to come inside.

I again felt apprehensive, so I picked up my camera and tripod and went back into the bedroom, locking the patio door. I would still have plenty of time to take night photos, so I would listen to him and go inside. I was sure the buffalo would soon go on down to the creek.

I sat on the bed, and Mambo jumped up by my side. He was still shaking, so I talked to him and petted him for awhile, and then turned my camera on to look at the photos I'd taken.

My night sky shots were great, and after I got home and fiddled with them on my computer, I was sure they would be impressive. The camera had captured layer after layer of stars, including distant gasses of different colors. It was an expensive camera and lens, and I'd been hesitant to buy it, but now I was very happy I had.

I next scanned to the shots of the buffalo, but they were fuzzy and out of focus, and I really couldn't make out much except a pair of reddish-gold eyes looking straight at me. Most animal eyes are yellow when caught by light in the dark, but I thought that maybe a buffalo's eyes were more reddish.

I set my camera down when something dawned on me. I'd been in Grand Teton National Park a couple of summers before, talking with the ranger about animal eyeshine. It was a fascinating discussion, and one thing she told me suddenly resurfaced in my mind as I stood there, wondering what was outside.

The ranger had told me that ungulates like deer, elk, sheep, and mountain goats have their eyes on the sides of their heads so they can keep a good lookout for predators. She said that if you ever see a pair of close-set eyes looking at you, you know you're looking at a predator, a situation where you would be wise to flee.

What I'd seen outside was no buffalo! I again studied the photos in my camera, and sure enough, both eyes were close together, looking straight at me. They had to both be in the front of the head, a head that must be quite large to have eyes that size.

I shivered. What was out there? Were there bears in this area? It made sense, as Notom seemed to be in a transition zone between desert and mountains, and the Henrys weren't far away.

I pushed the button by the bed and brought the mechanized shades down, then got into my pajamas and crawled into bed. Mambo usually sleeps at my feet, but he was still shaking and wanted down under the covers, so I let him. Labradors aren't known for being aggressive, but I was surprised at how afraid he was.

I didn't sleep well that night, tossing and turning, and Mambo shook for a long time before he finally went to sleep. I was hyper alert, listening for any sounds, but there was nothing.

The next day was bright and sunny, and I decided it would be good to get out and drive through Capital Reef National Park, since it was right in my backyard. The house sat right on the park boundary, but the main visitor area was further down the highway another 10 miles or so.

I would go see the main sights, then drive into the nearby town of Torrey and look around. I wouldn't be able to do any hiking since dogs weren't allowed on the park trails, which I found ironic, since I could hike directly into the park right out my back door with Mambo and no one would ever know. I would get a map while there to see where we could hike once back at the house.

The park was gorgeous, even though there were lots of people. I bought a couple of books at the Visitor Center about the geology and animals, giving me something to do at night.

But the best part of the day was visiting the little town of Torrey, especially the book store, where I bought even more books. It was too hot to leave Mambo in the car for long, so I didn't dally. I then took him for a hike down to the Fremont River, where he splashed around and dived underwater for rocks, as silly Labs will do. I could tell he was happy to be away from the house, or was I imagining it?

Was I the one who was actually happy to be away? What a strange thought, and I pondered it as I drove back to the house. Nothing was making me stay. I could leave anytime I wanted. Why would I even think such a thing? It was an awesome house in an even more awesome setting. I wasn't going to let things that go bump in the night worry me.

I'd really enjoyed the day, but the minute I turned back onto the Notom Road, a feeling of oppression hit me. It didn't help that I ran into Will again, riding along the road, and he told me he'd found yet another of his missing calves, this one down by the creek.

I asked if it had been a victim of the flash flood, but he said no. I realized that I was beginning to not want to talk to him, and I knew it was a "shoot the messenger" thing, as he always had something unsettling to tell me. He was putting a damper on my vacation, even though it wasn't his fault. I decided not to mention what I'd seen the previous night.

I got home and let Mambo inside when it dawned on me that I should go look where the bear or whatever it was had been, as maybe I'd find tracks. I grabbed my camera.

Yes, there were indeed tracks, and lots of them, tracks just like I'd seen around the calf, tracks that pushed deep into the sand from something heavy, tracks with toes, as if someone barefoot was walking around, someone really big. I took lots of photos.

Now I was having second thoughts. Maybe I should go tell Will what I'd seen and show him my photos. It was getting on towards evening, and the thought of being alone in the house after dark was becoming unsettling.

I fed Mambo his dinner, then took him out for a little evening walk, feeling more than a bit apprehensive and looking over my shoulder. I could tell he felt the same, eager to get back to the house, so we turned around.

I ate the leftovers from my lunch in Torrey, then opened one of the books I'd bought, but I couldn't get that interested in it. I thought about trying to take some more night shots, but I just wasn't in the mood.

It was almost dark when I heard the sound of a vehicle pulling up in front of the house. I opened the door and saw a brown pickup that had seen better days. It had a few bales of hay in the bed and a gun rack in the back window. I could see that Will was driving it, and he had a passenger.

I walked out and said hello, Mambo at my heels. Will introduced me to his wife, Mary, then said they'd just come up to check on me and make sure everything was all right.

They'd found yet another calf that afternoon and were worried that whatever was doing it might not stop there, whatever that meant. I could tell that they were really nice people and well-meaning, but all this worrying was putting me on edge, and I needed the opposite, to relax.

"You know where we live, don't you dear?" Mary asked. "If you get even a bit nervous or hear anything unusual, you come on down. We have a spare bedroom, and your dog is more than welcome."

I was hesitant, but decided it would be good to show them the tracks, so we walked over by the house. I didn't mention that I'd actually seen whatever had made them. Neither had much to say, but they looked grim, then again offered their spare bedroom.

Finally, Mary said, "I'm not sure it's a good idea for you to be here alone. Why don't you just come on down to our place? Will said you were just visiting. It might be a good idea to cut your visit short. I really don't want to scare you, but we're having some really odd things happen around here lately."

I decided not to mention my photos of the eyes. In all honesty, I was very nervous, but going back to the city early was not something I wanted to do. I'd paid to stay in the house, and I wanted to enjoy it. Surely what was going on had to do with their cattle, not me. Some kind of predator was enjoying the easy pickings.

It was a quiet night, and I went to bed early, tired from the busy day. Even though my first few nights there I'd wanted the shades closed, this night was different. I wanted to lounge in bed and look at the stars, reveling in their beauty. I fell asleep as if I were cradled in a soft bed of blue-white diamonds. I'll never forget that feeling of complete solace.

I woke early to a colorful sunrise and stood on the deck taking photo after photo, again happy to be there. All my trepidation had faded, and I felt a sense of exultation. There was no other way to describe the feeling of being in such an awesome place while having the warmth and security of a house. The only time I'd ever been out in wilderness like that was tent camping, which quickly got uncomfortable and tiresome.

I decided it would be a good day to take my new map and head to the backside of the park, the area right out my door. The map showed the park boundary was just across Pleasant Creek. I would pretty much just hike parallel to the park, as I really didn't want to break the rules and take Mambo where he shouldn't be.

I put my camera and lunch in a day pack, along with water and snacks, and off we went. The creek crossing was easy, and I could actually step from stone to stone without getting my feet wet. There was a lot of debris washed up high on the banks from the flash flood.

I threw a stick into the creek for Mambo for awhile, and even though he didn't want to leave the water, he finally followed me as we headed toward the big sandstone domes in the park.

We wound our way through what looked like huge alluvial fans, although it was really just the eroded remnants of what had once been on top of the domes. At one point, we climbed a long hill and I could see the Golden Throne, one of the park's landmarks, a huge white dome with golden sandstone on its shoulders.

It was on this hill that I found a number of native workings, chips and flakes from making spear points and arrowheads. I knew that the Fremont people roamed this country, contemporaries of the Anasazi or Ancestral Puebloans, and I wondered if they enjoyed the view as much as I did.

Finally, I could tell Mambo was really starting to feel the heat, so we turned around. July was not the best time to be in the canyon country, and even though we'd gotten an early start, it was quickly warming up.

We were soon back at Pleasant Creek, where we ate our lunches and played in the water. I threw Mambo a stick over and over, and finally quit when I could tell he was getting tired. I think Labs would play stick until they actually keeled over.

But as we climbed up the bank, I saw something that was truly chilling. I could make out our tracks coming down from the house and crossing the damp bank, and next to them were the same huge tracks I'd seen over by the calf and then later by the house.

But what made this so especially worrisome was that in places the tracks veered directly on top of my own—whatever it was, it'd been following us. It could be watching us right now from behind the cottonwoods along the creek.

I'd been letting Mambo run free, but I quickly clipped his leash onto his harness and took off for the house, afraid to look behind us. Once there, I locked the door and collapsed into the recliner. It took me awhile to recover, but I finally got up and got a cold drink from the refrigerator, wondering what to do.

I'd only been there a few days, and I'd paid a pretty good amount to stay there, but maybe Will and Mary were right and I should leave. Things were getting just a bit too personal when you found scary tracks superimposed on your own.

I tried to be reasonable, thinking maybe whatever it was had just gone down to get a drink and it was a coincidence that its tracks were on top of mine, but something told me I was kidding myself.

The ranger's words came back to me, "If you ever see a pair of close-set eyes looking at you, you know you're looking at a predator, a situation where you would be wise to flee."

This thing was a predator, there was no doubt in my mind. It had obviously killed Will's calves, and now I had evidence that it had been tracking me. On top of that, it had been lurking just outside the house, watching me. It could've followed me every time I took Mambo out, which would explain his trepidation. His senses were much better than mine, and I knew I should be listening more carefully to him.

Mambo was at my feet, as usual, shaking, and that's when it struck me. I could be cavalier with what I did, as I was responsible for my own choices in life, but I was also responsible for *his* life, and I didn't want to do anything that might bring him harm. Maybe I was being stubborn by staying. Maybe it was indeed time to leave.

Hiking in the heat had worn me out, and I soon fell asleep there in the big leather recliner. When I woke, it was late afternoon, and I decided it was time to listen to my intuition and go.

I would get a room at Hanna's motel, spend a day or two there, then find someplace else to go for the rest of my vacation. Maybe they would refund my money, but if not, I would just write off the cost of the house.

I had a late lunch, then started gathering my stuff. I didn't have much, but I put my suitcase and a few things in the car, then tried to take Mambo out for a quick break, but he refused to go. All that I had left was my overnight stuff upstairs, where I'd also left my camera gear.

I went upstairs to get it all, then stood on the deck for a moment to say my last farewell to the incredible views. It was then that I changed my mind. I'd never seen a night sky so thick with so many stars—I would stay just one more night and get as many photos as possible, then leave first thing in the morning.

I knew in my gut that I should go, but I chose to ignore my intuition. It later became a valuable lesson to me, something I will never do again. Like I mentioned at the beginning of this story, this whole thing seriously traumatized me, but it was the night to come that did the real damage.

I again set up my camera on the deck, Mambo at my feet. Since it was earlier than the last time I'd tried to take shots, Sagittarius was at more of an angle to the deck, so I had to pull my tripod way over into the corner to get it all in view.

I took a few test shots, which looked fine, so I decided to use my intervalometer, which I could set to trigger the shutter at specific times, saving me the trouble of standing and waiting.

An intervalometer is the same type of device that tells your automatic sprinklers to go on and off and is used a lot in night photography. My camera had one built into it, which made it really easy to set up and then go do something else while the camera took photos.

I set it to trigger a shot every 20 seconds, then turned to enjoy the sight of the immense bowl of stars over me. It was then that I noticed that Mambo had curled himself into the corner of the deck near the camera, and was again shaking.

I looked all around the yard in front of the house but could see nothing, which was to be expected, since it was pitch dark. But now I heard something new—it sounded like something was on the roof of the house, a sort of creaking noise as if something heavy was walking across the fiberglass shingles.

A bolt of terror shot through me, followed by a shot of adrenaline. We needed to get inside!

It was too late, for I could see a large black head just above where I was standing, and before even thinking about it, I had dived into the corner of the deck, hiding down on my knees next to Mambo.

Just a split second later, something huge came crashing down onto the deck, making it shake, then went through the patio door. For some reason, it hadn't seen us!

It was hard to make out much, but whatever it was, it walked on two legs and was very heavy and dark. My first reaction was that it went inside to look for food, but a terror quickly rose inside me, telling me it was looking for me and Mambo. We had to get away!

Mambo was still wearing the harness I'd put on him for our last walk, and even though he was a good-sized dog, he was in good shape and light on his feet.

The roof continued on past the corner of the deck where we hid, and I carefully lifted Mambo up onto it, holding for dear life onto his harness, then pulled myself up and slowly walked us both to where the roof slanted down close to the ground.

We were still a good eight feet up. I was pretty light and could probably jump without injuring myself, but I didn't think Mambo could land as easily. It then dawned on me that if I went ahead and jumped, got into my car and drove over under the roof, I could stand on it and pull him down. I would have to work fast. In retrospect, I don't know what I was thinking, for I should've just pulled him off with me, as he was light and would've been fine.

I told him to stay, then jumped, landing harder than I expected, a bit jolted but uninjured. I made a mad dash for my car when I realized my keys were inside on the kitchen counter. I was stunned. There was no way I could go back inside the house, and I expected the creature to come out the moment it realized we weren't in there.

I was now happy that the house had no curtains, for I could see the entire living room and kitchen, and the creature wasn't downstairs yet.

I would have to sneak in, grab my keys, and get back out before it came down. I couldn't recall if I'd locked the house, but since I'd been loading my stuff, I didn't think I had.

The very thought of going inside made my knees weak, but I had no choice. I couldn't just leave Mambo up on the roof, and if I didn't get the car and rescue him, that's where he would be stuck. If the creature found him, well, it would be truly horrible. He would end up like those calves, I was sure.

I quietly slipped the front door open, quickly moving into the kitchen and grabbing my keys off the counter, then was back outside in a flash. There was still no sign of the creature, and I wondered if the spiral staircase wasn't keeping it upstairs, as it was so big.

I could now hear Mambo whining. Darn! He was going to give away his location. Why had I left him? I had to act fast.

I ran to the car and started it, then drove it right under the edge of the roof, leaving it running. I climbed up onto the top of the car, where I could see that Mambo had gone to the other edge of the roof, looking for me, still whining.

This was terrible! He hadn't stayed where I'd told him, and I knew we were running out of time. I called to him quietly, glad he was a mamma's boy as he came running over.

He was now on the roof just a few feet above me, but he wouldn't come down. It was only a few feet to jump, but he was too scared. I again called to him, telling him he was a good boy and reassuring him, and just as he jumped onto the car's roof, I saw a large figure come out onto the deck.

I pushed Mambo into the car and jumped in behind him just as something slammed against it, actually knocking it a bit askew. I gunned it, sand and rocks flying through the air, and I could see a large dark creature in my rear-view mirror, reaching out to grab at us.

I was too afraid to look behind me again until I was clear down on the main road, heading for the highway, but at that point, I'd fortunately left the creature far behind.

I didn't stop until I got to Hannah's motel in Hanksville. By then, it was late, and it didn't look like there was anyone in the office, so I sat there in my car for the longest time, me and Mambo both shaking. It took awhile to realize that I was now safe, and at that point I started sobbing.

I have no idea how long I sat there, but finally I saw someone come into the office and turn off the vacancy sign. It was Hannah. She saw me and came out, quite surprised, asking me if there was something wrong.

I literally could not talk. Hannah helped me and Mambo into one of the motel rooms, where, to her credit, she sat with me all night as I sobbed myself to sleep. It wasn't until the next morning that I could tell her why I was there, and then not in much detail.

I basically stayed in the room all the next day, mustering the courage to take Mambo out once in awhile, but not wanting to go anywhere else. Hannah brought me takeout from the nearby restaurant, and I was finally able to tell her in more detail what happened.

I was worried she wouldn't believe me, but she was very patient, and I spent the following night on her couch, as I didn't want to be alone. Mambo slept, as usual, at my feet, and he seemed to be recovering better than I was.

The following day, both Hannah and her husband drove me back to the Notom house, and I noticed they had a rifle in the back of the car. Frankly, I was happy for it.

Mambo stayed at their house in Hanksville with their dog, Goldie, where he managed to get into my suitcase and drag around one of my shirts, basically ruining it. I think he needed the comfort it brought, but it also looked as if he and Goldie had played tug-of-war with it, which I didn't mind, as it meant he was feeling better.

When we arrived at the Notom house, I had no idea if the creature had damaged anything or not, but everything was as it should be, except the bedroom door was open out onto the deck and the house had an odd odor to it. My camera still sat on the tripod just as I'd left it.

It was all I could do to go back inside and gather my stuff. Hannah locked up the house, and we all went straight back to Hanksville. Hannah knew Will and Mary and said she would call them later, as she felt they needed to know what was going on.

She also felt that the homeowners would give me a refund for the time I had remaining at the house, especially after hearing what had happened. She said she was now suspecting they'd left for the same reason I had, thinking back on a few comments they'd made.

At that point, all I wanted to do was go home, so I went back to Salt Lake. I spent the next two weeks pretty much locked away, trying to process everything that I'd seen, but not having much luck. I decided to schedule some time with a therapist, but I chickened out, worrying that no one would believe me. Given my profession, having something this odd on my record might come back to haunt me.

I knew Hannah believed me, and she and I had a number of good phone conversations, which helped me immensely. She did call Will and Mary, but they had nothing new to report.

I didn't talk to Hannah again for some time, but when I did, she told me that she and her husband were moving to Colorado, as they'd sold the motel.

The same people who bought it had also bought the Notom house, even though she'd told them my story. They of course weren't sure if they believed it, and were going to turn the house into a bed and breakfast. If my story were true, they would use it to market the house as being on the edge of true strangeness, which they were sure would bring lots of business. I wasn't so sure about that, but I said nothing, wondering what Will and Mary would think.

It was probably a good month before I downloaded the photos on my camera. There were a lot more than I expected, as the interval-ometer had triggered the shutter for several hours until the battery finally died.

Most of the shots were of the night sky, and some were really spectacular. In fact, after running them through my photo-editing program, I will say some were good enough to enlarge and frame, which I did, putting several on my walls.

But a few of the earlier photos told a story. There were several star photos, then I could barely make out the shape of something standing right in front of the camera, something with a strange texture, which I took to be out-of-focus hair.

The camera then went back to taking star photos, but after awhile, there was again something in front of it, but this time far enough away from the camera that it was more in focus. I figured that this was when the creature had gone out onto the roof looking for us.

I had a photo of the back of a large black head, and I knew this was taken just before the creature jumped off the deck, the moment before it slammed into my car.

None of the photos had the clarity or focus to convince anyone of anything, except me, but only because I'd seen it in reality. I tried to work through the trauma of what had happened, but every time I looked at the photos it seemed to return.

I eventually deleted them all, including the video of the flash flood, and I even deleted the shots of the night sky. I gave the photos I'd framed to friends. I needed to clear my head and forget that I'd ever been to the Notom house.

I soon left my job and followed Hannah and her husband to Colorado, where I got a job in a bank. That's where I met my future husband, and we moved onto on a small acreage near town.

Mambo loved the nearby lakes and streams there and lived to be an old gray-muzzled dog, but I sometimes wondered if he didn't dream of the Notom house, for he would occasionally wake and come to me, shaking, looking for comfort.

I now have two kids, and even though we like to visit the national parks on our family vacations, I'm very careful about where we stay.

I know what's out there, and if I have my way, I'll be sure that my family never does.

6

MOUNTAIN MADNESS

I met Dan on a fly-fishing trip on the Beaverhead River near Dillon, Montana, one of my favorite rivers, having the biggest brown trout in the state. Dan was a stellar fisherman, though he was very quiet, but that's OK, as we were out there to fish, not talk up a storm.

Later, over one of my dutch-oven dinners, I noted that the others seemed comfortable, but Dan pretty much kept to himself. But just before he left to go back to his home in Missoula, he asked me if I would call him the next time I was in the area.

I just happened to be going that way a few weeks later to take a group to fish the Bitterroot, and he invited me to his house. It had some of the most beautiful woodwork I've ever seen, and he told me he'd done all the work himself and was getting ready to sell it and go back to California.

He then told me he would like to share something that happened to him, if I had the time. Well, I always have the time to listen to Bigfoot stories, short or long. I found out that he was an interesting guy, as was his story.
—Rusty

Rusty, to be honest, the only reason I'm able to tell you this is because I've read enough of your books to believe that more people than I'd realized have had strange encounters like mine. The one thing most of their stories have in common is that they've been changed by what they've seen. I know I was.

I think part of the change is acknowledging that you're not the invincible person you thought you were. I mean, I used to go out and not be afraid of anything, and I have to admit I was kind of proud of that persona.

I was the brave mountaineer who could see my way through anything—it was a kind of pride, and I was hard on my climbing partners, overly critical. But after all this happened, I don't climb anymore, and I try to be kinder now, more tolerant.

But let me tell you why I don't climb. Bear with me, as it's a long story.

Ever since I was a kid I had the urge to climb things. It all started out with an interest in insects, believe it or not. When I was little, I would collect bugs and study them. My greatest treasure was a microscope that my parents got me when I was about six.

Well, I lived in the Sierras, so my bug hunting usually involved climbing a hill or two, or even occasional small cliffs. As time went on, I would go further and further afield, climbing more and more, until by the time I was in high school I was climbing mountains with friends for the sake of the climbing itself, not to find bugs.

Well, my mom had high hopes that I would go to college and get a degree and teach at a university. I hated to disappoint her, but I gradually lost my interest in bugs, which was replaced by wanting to do nothing but climb.

Strangely enough, my interest in bugs rubbed off on one of my school buddies, and he became an entomology researcher who specialized in high-altitude insects, probably making his mom very proud.

Sometimes, if I saw an unusual bug when I was out climbing, I would catch it and send it to him for his collection. He would actually sometimes cite me in his papers as a research partner, which was pretty generous. I would always show these to my mom, which was kind of pathetic, in retrospect.

But I ended up becoming a carpenter, which fit perfectly with my desire to climb, as I could work as I saw fit, as opposed to having a full-time job I had to go to every day. My sister became a community college teacher, which kind of assuaged my mom's desire for her kids to amount to something, at least by her standards.

I never talked about my climbing to my family, and I doubt if they had any idea that I was eventually considered a top climber, with a number of first ascents. I knew that my climbing worried my parents, so I just never talked about it, even though it was all I lived for. Almost every extra penny I made went to finance my climbs, although I did buy an old house and started working on it.

I had a couple of climbing partners, depending on who could get away when, but I liked climbing with my good friend Chris the best. Chris was actually one of my old high-school buddies, and we'd been climbing together for years. Like me, Chris was a low achiever when it came to employment, working odd jobs and whatever he could find when he wasn't out in the mountains.

He was what we call a dirtbag, someone who sacrifices everything for their passion, and he lived in his old VW bus, though he sometimes slept in my enclosed porch when the weather got bad.

I technically wasn't a dirtbag because I was self-employed and had a house that I could return to after each climb. I'd bought it for almost nothing and fixed it up as time went along, though it sure wasn't fancy. This house was in Missoula, Montana, where Chris and I had moved when we were younger, as it seemed like a good central base for climbing the U.S. and Canadian Rockies.

Chris was pretty well-known in the climbing world, much more so than I was. He had actually even been featured in a few climbing magazines. Our styles were different, which is part of what made us good partners. He was somewhat serendipitous, and I was very methodical.

Well, Chris and I may not have been particularly ambitious in the corporate sense of the word, but we sure were when it came to climbing and peak bagging. We'd decided it would be a worthy goal to climb all 10 of the highest peaks in North America. This was a pretty big goal just based on what it would cost us to get to them, let alone the effort and skill it would take to actually climb them.

We'd climbed two, Denali and Foraker, the highest and sixth highest, when we decided we were ready for the second highest, which is Mount Logan in Canada, in Yukon Territory to be specific.

Logan stands at 19,551 feet, only 759 feet shorter than Denali, and is also second in North America after Denali for prominence, which is the distance from base to top.

Compared to Denali, Mt. Logan's not a real difficult mountain to climb, other than the preparation and necessary stamina. You do need to be well-practiced in crevasse rescue though, because the mountain is surrounded by big glaciers full of treacherous crevasses. It's not a technical climb, but you won't see as many people up there like on Denali because Logan's fairly inaccessible.

Logan's very isolated, cold, high, and gets really crazy weather any time of the year, as storms can come off the Gulf of Alaska and bring major blizzards, even in the summer. I read somewhere that the weather on Mt. Logan made the weather on Denali look like a summer breeze. Denali's famous for its bad weather, so that was really saying something.

We'd flown into Anchorage the time we climbed Denali and Foraker, but because we were both pretty broke, we decided to try to save money by driving up to the Yukon from Montana.

To make a long story short, it took us almost three weeks to get there, one of which was spent sitting in Whitehorse waiting for parts to arrive. Chris's bus broke down twice, and I swear it couldn't go over 50 m.p.h. without shaking. And every time he turned it off, I worried that it wouldn't start again.

Well, we finally left Whitehorse, drove through the little village of Haines Junction, then got to Kluane Lake, one of the most beautiful places ever, with the white-topped St. Elias Range, which holds Mt. Logan, towering above the lake to the west. We stopped at a pullover and had lunch, neither of us saying a word. We knew we were in for the climb of a lifetime.

We couldn't see Logan from where we were, but we knew it was back in there somewhere, the crown jewel of Kluane National Park and Reserve. Because it's in the southeast corner of the park, far from any trailhead or road, few people have ever seen it, as it's a good two-day hike to get to where it's even visible.

Of course, you can fly over it, but that's not the same, for you don't capture the wild feeling you get by actually being there. Had the border been drawn a few more miles to the east, the mountain would've been in the United States.

The Logan Massif is the world's largest ice sheet that's not part of an ice cap, a huge plateau with a dozen peaks rising from it with ridges and summits that have never been climbed, the largest mountain in the world by base circumference. The other peaks bear names like Teddy Peak, Queen Peak, King's Peak, Catenary Peak, and Prospector's Peak.

The climb to the top of Logan can be a two to three week undertaking from the base to the summit, and longer if you have to sit out bad weather. Some people have taken a month to climb it.

Anyway, while we were sitting at the rest area, a guy on a road bike came riding up, panniers stuffed to the gills. He was from Bulgaria and was riding all the way from Fairbanks to Argentina.

We gave him some water, and he told us about being chased on his bike by a grizzly bear right down the middle of the highway only a few miles back. His face was still flushed, and he kept looking up the road. It kind of brought home that we were in truly wild country.

Chris and I finally left the rest area, following the highway along the shore of the huge lake, finally coming to the small settlement of Burwash Landing, where we would charter a plane.

We'd talked to the charter company a week before and they'd said we didn't need a reservation, as things were pretty slow. We'd been afraid to make a commitment, the way things were going with the bus, as we had no idea when we would arrive.

Well, come to find out, it was a good thing we hadn't made a reservation, because we'd totally forgotten to stop in Haines Junction to pick up our climbing permits. We turned around.

Chris was laughing, taking it as just another element of the grand adventure, whereas I was a bit more somber. It seemed like a lot had gone wrong already, and I wondered what was to come. I hoped our bad luck would end once we got on the mountain.

We were soon in Haines Junction at the headquarters for Kluane National Park and Reserve. The building was reminiscent of most Forest Service buildings I'd seen in the United States, but since it was Sunday, it was closed, something else we hadn't anticipated.

Because it sat back on the edge of town and was fairly private, Chris and I decided to just sleep there in his bus in the parking lot. It helped that there was a little bakery right across the street where we could get coffee and lunch.

As we sat there in the bus eating blueberry pie, the bakery's specialty, we decided on a change of plans. We would pick up our climbing permit, which we'd had to apply for three months before our arrival (part of the reason we'd forgotten about it), then charter a bush plane there in Haines Junction instead of going all the way back to Burwash Landing.

At this point, we just wanted to be on the flanks of Logan. We were burning through our money, what with fixing the old bus and taking so long, so we wanted to get to our destination before anything else went wrong. I had deeper pockets than Chris and had paid the $600 it had cost to fix the bus, and I was despairing of ever getting to our destination.

That late June night there in the parking lot, surrounded by trees and quiet, was one of the nicest nights I've ever spent in a town. Granted, Haines Junction is pretty small, but I think part of the ambience I felt was from knowing that the old bus had finally gotten us there. If I'd had any idea what was to come, I probably would've been awake all night.

But we both slept well, then went inside in the morning and got our climbing permits. We also had to buy wilderness backcountry permits, as well as pay an aircraft landing fee, but none of it added up to a lot. The real costs would be in chartering the plane, which we finally scheduled. We would fly out the next day.

We had quite a few questions for the rangers there, and they told us a lot about the mountain and previous climbs, but the one thing that struck me as odd was when one of them told us not to cache food. It seemed that this season, something had been eating everyone's caches, putting a number of climbers in tricky situations without provisions. We would have to carry everything we needed with us or risk losing it.

At Denali, we'd had the folks at the Talkeetna air charter drop a cache for us at the 14,400 foot camp so we wouldn't have to carry it up, which had been an immense help, even though with just the two of us, we didn't need as many supplies as a big expedition.

We'd hoped to do something similar here, so this was bad news. We would just have to climb as fast as we could and be careful so we wouldn't run out of food.

"Who'd be low enough to steal someone's cache?" I asked.

"We don't know," the ranger replied. "As you know, a climber will only dip into someone else's cache in an emergency, when it's life or death. But so far this season every time someone leaves a cache, it's disappeared—and not just part of it, but the entire thing, vanished with no trace. We've had to make several emergency rescues because of this. If you find out who's doing it, we would love to know."

"Could it be a bear?" Chris asked.

"It's highly unlikely, as bears on Logan are unheard of. It's just too high and extreme for most animals, even marmots, who will steal food, but not an entire cache. And all animals will leave trash behind when they steal food."

Chris and I discussed this later, deciding it had to be a bear, regardless of what the ranger thought. We'd heard of bears at high altitudes, though Logan would be a bit extreme, but if a bear managed to climb up high enough and found a cache, it might be likely to just hang around if there were more to be found. Maybe it had a secret hiding place where it would rummage through every-thing and leave the trash. It could end up staying up there until the climbing season was over, which was usually by the end of July, then head back down.

And as I thought more about it, I recalled reading a book where an Alaskan bush pilot had said he'd seen wolves, grizzly, lynx, and black bears at altitudes of 10,000 feet. Who knows, maybe they went even higher. The pilot had also said he'd seen ravens riding thermals at 17,000 feet, and ravens were notorious for stealing food, though they usually left a mess of wrappers.

Chris and I both knew that a bear in that high expanse of snow and glacial ice and crevasses would be living dangerously. Logan wasn't bear's play as mountains go. Even experienced Himalayan climbers were impressed by Logan, saying they thought they'd seen gigantic peaks until they had their first glimpse of the massif. For a bear to even climb up there would be pretty much unthinkable, and why would it even want to?

We had an entire day to kill before flying in, so we basically just hung around town, talking to people at the local gear shop and trying to find out more about the mountain.

I was glad we'd gone to the shop because they talked us into buying a toboggan, or glacier sled, which made transporting our gear much easier. As with everything else, I paid for it.

I could pull the sled and ease a lot of the load from my pack, plus we could stock up on more supplies, making the trip ultimately safer. Chris was ambivalent about the purchase, and I knew he was worrying about money. Even though I ended up moaning bitterly about having to drag the sled, I was ultimately glad I'd bought it.

We ended up in a local bar that night against my wishes, but Chris wanted to celebrate getting this far. I told him we would cele-brate when we got back off the mountain, but he was the kind of guy who didn't need much to justify a good brew.

I noted, ironically, that he wasn't all that worried about spending his cash on alcohol, and the last thing I wanted was a climbing partner with a hangover, but I also didn't want to spoil his fun. So, I begrudgingly went along, figuring it would be better than sitting alone in the old bus. I like a nice cold beer myself, but not when I'm getting ready to climb. Besides, I knew Chris would get hammered, as he always did.

But that's where I met Kim. She was part of a group of five Canadians who were also going to start up Logan the next day. Like me, she looked like she would rather be somewhere else than in a bar, maybe reading a book.

We really hit it off. She was from Edmonton and was small and lithe, yet looked like someone who could easily pull her own weight. She had a warmth that really made one feel at ease.

She told me she was a nurse, and her fellow climbers worked at the same hospital she did. Two were doctors, one was a lab technician, and another was a fellow nurse. She was the only woman on the expedition, and I could tell that her fellow team members thought highly of her.

Well, it was getting late, and even though I was enjoying talking to Kim, it was time to drag Chris back to the bus and get some sleep. He was out the minute he hit his sleeping bag, but I couldn't sleep. At first I thought about Kim and how nice she was, then I started thinking again about all the problems that had plagued this trip.

Like I said earlier, Chris and I had been climbing partners since high school, but this entire trip it seemed like our relationship was souring a bit, and I wasn't sure why. Both of us had been out of sorts and snappy since we'd left Montana, and his bus breaking down hadn't helped things.

When I would complain, he would snap right back, saying he'd supplied the transportation, as unreliable as it was. I reminded him that I was paying the gas, which was much more than I'd planned, as the bus was a gas hog. At one point I was ready to turn around and go back, but we finally managed to patch things up.

Now, as Chris snored next to me, reeking of alcohol, I made a decision—this would be our last climb together. It seemed that we'd both turned into grouchy old men, even though we were both only in our 40's—but for climbers, we were getting long in the tooth.

I was again thinking about Kim, and I decided I would try to get her address if we met again on the mountain, assuming she was single. I must be getting old, I mused, if the thought of climbing took second place to getting a woman's phone number. Maybe I was ready to settle down. I had the feeling Chris was also burning out.

After all, we'd made a good run at things, so why not retire from the big peaks and enjoy something else, something not so dangerous? Maybe trying to climb the top 10 peaks was too ambitious. I'd always wanted to build my own cabin up in the Sierras—maybe I'd sell the Montana house and go do that, go back home. I knew my parents would like that, and they were getting elderly.

As I lay there, sleepless, my mind drifted to the first winter expedition on Denali in 1967, still called McKinley at that time.

The eight-man expedition had lost one member to a crevasse and been plagued with bad weather and marginal choices, even though it had successfully put three of the group on the summit.

Those three had spent over a week in a small snow cave at 18,000 feet in 150 m.p.h. winds with wind chills of nearly minus 150 degrees, with only enough food for two days. Most of the team had suffered frostbite, some serious, and a helicopter rescue had been necessary because of the frostbite and more incoming bad weather, even though they'd managed to get partway back down once the weather broke.

It struck me that the only reason the three near the top had survived was because they'd managed to dig into an old frozen cache, where they'd found enough food to carry them over until the winds died down. They had literally been starving until they found it.

The leader, highly experienced and a strong climber, had later told the other team members that he'd been distracted and hadn't done his best, even though no one blamed him for what had been a series of mostly bad-luck circumstances. But he told them that all he could think about during the expedition was getting back home, for his priorities had changed.

There in the bus, I could feel the same kind of change. Maybe I should cancel tomorrow, tell Chris I didn't want to do the climb, and go home. If I was going to climb Logan, I wanted to do my best, and right now I wasn't feeling very enthusiastic.

I wasn't the leader of our little two-man expedition, neither of us was, but I somehow felt partly responsible for Chris. I then realized that what I was feeling was resentment—I'd always been the more responsible one, the one who worked hard and thereby had a porch for Chris to sleep on, the one who always had more money to pay for things.

Maybe I'd internalized my parent's values more than I realized, but I was beginning to feel that Chris took advantage of me and always had. I'd known this, of course, but this trip was really bringing it to the forefront of my thoughts, and I was tired of it after all these years.

I knew Chris would be angry if I bailed, but he might be able to sign on with Kim's group. They'd seemed to take to one another at the bar, and Chris was a good-natured guy with top-notch experience. He would be a great asset to any climbing party. I could hitch a ride back to Whitehorse and fly home. I would leave Chris enough gas money to get back, since that was part of the deal.

I finally drifted off in peace, deciding I wouldn't climb Logan after all. It seemed the perfect solution to my worries, and as I drifted off, I wondered again who or what was stealing the caches.

Of course, the next morning I was back to my old self, all worries gone, excited to make the trip, hoping to meet Kim on the trail. Chris was hungover, but he always recovered, though I'd noticed as he aged it seemed to take longer and he grumbled more.

In another twist of irony, after we'd confirmed and paid for the air charter, we found out the airport was near Burwash Landing, where we'd just been, but now we would have to pay for a shuttle from Haines Junction. More cash out the window—my cash.

But we were soon in the air, and after awhile, we could see the Logan Massif in the distance. It soared far above the surrounding glaciers and peaks, seeming to completely occupy the horizon, even from a long ways off. It looked surreal, beautiful, and intimidating—and very stark and lonely.

The yellow Helio Courier set us down at the Mt. Logan basecamp on the Quintino Sella Glacier at about 9,000 feet. We were now on a vast white expanse of snow at King's Trench, named for nearby 16,972-foot King's Peak, the ninth tallest mountain in North America.

The King's Trench route ascends the west side of Logan and is non-technical, and one can ski most of its large glacier system, though it's interlaced with crevasses and avalanche danger. Like most climbers, we would follow the trench, climb to the great plateau where the summit block stood, then make our way to the top—hopefully, anyway.

We'd landed not too far from Kim and her friends. We unloaded our gear, and I carefully lashed part of it onto the sled. I'd thought that maybe we would take turns pulling it, but Chris refused to put any of his gear on it, saying it was just going to be a nuisance.

I was again irritated but said nothing, putting on my skis, knowing that he would be happy to eat some of the extra food on the sled when the need arose.

Since it was still early, we decided to head out and hopefully make good time. Most people stay at least one night at the basecamp to help acclimate, but we wanted to get going, to get as far as we could in case we were later plagued with some of the bad weather the massif was famous for.

We had left Kim's group in the dust, so to speak, and we camped that night under a rock ridge, tired but happy. Chris wanted to try to get to the King's Trench Camp, only 2,000 feet above, but I'd argued that we'd be better off taking it easy and just going a short distance, getting our legs under us, so to speak.

Besides, getting all the way to the King's Trench Camp meant crossing a field with crevasse danger, and I wanted to cross it early in the morning, when the light was better and one could maybe make out places where the snow was thinner, potentially hiding crevasses.

We pitched our two-man tent, then I set up our little stove and boiled water, which seemed to take forever at that altitude. We had a dinner of freeze-dried stew with raisins, followed by cups of hot jello, and then glops of peanut butter and dark chocolate all melted together in hot black tea.

It was imperative to drink lots of fluids so we didn't get dehydrated, for at those altitudes one tended not to get thirsty, even though your body still needed plenty of water.

Finally satiated, Chris and I now kicked back, our sleeping pads under us, leaning against our tent and watching a fiery sunset down King's Trench. It was 11 p.m., and even though it was midsummer, we were far enough north that the sky never really did get dark.

I finally went to bed, all our gear pulled up into the tent's vestibule with the toboggan stuck into the snow, serving as a kind of door. I thought again of something stealing caches, but I couldn't begin to imagine what could exist out in this vast whiteness of snow and ice.

It was beginning to get light again at four a.m., and even though I wasn't completely rested, I was up and about, melting more snow for water.

We were soon moving, Chris breaking trail with his skis and me following along, the ends of my skis getting bound up in the toboggan lines and even slamming against the front edge of the sled at times.

It was frustrating, but I refused to say anything to Chris, as I didn't want him to think he'd been right. In a way, the sled made things easier, as it took the weight off my back and also allowed us to bring more supplies, but it seemed I was always getting tangled up in it. I'd heard of people's sleds getting free and taking off down the mountain, so I carried my pack, keeping everything I needed for survival in it, like my sleeping bag and the stove and fuel.

Even though it was only the second day, the whole thing was already beginning to feel like an endless slog. We were now going slower, knowing it was critically important to acclimate to the altitude. Neither of us had ever had any of the many disorders that go with high altitude climbing, such as pulmonary edema, but we'd known of others who hadn't made it back off the mountain.

We figured it would take us about 10 days to get to the actual summit if all went well and the weather was perfect, and part of that had to be spent acclimating, letting our bodies get used to the lack of oxygen. At this point, we were roped together, well aware of the crevasse dangers, taking it slow and easy.

That evening we made it to the King's Trench Camp, much more fatigued than we'd anticipated. We'd both climbed lots of 14,000-foot peaks in Colorado, yet this felt different, even though we were at only 11,000 feet. Everything seemed much more difficult, and I knew it was from the bitter cold, a minus 10° F by Chris's thermometer. I couldn't imagine how cold in must get up there in the winter.

I once again got out the stove and started melting snow, but just as the water started to boil, Chris took the pan and tossed the water into the air.

"What are you doing?" I asked, irritated.

"Look, Buckaroo, it froze instantly! Hey, take a picture!" he demanded.

Ever since I'd spent a summer in my youth working on a ranch in Colorado so I could climb there, Chris had called me Buckaroo, even though I'd never been on a horse.

I was now laughing. We had plenty of fuel, so I heated another pan of snow, and Chris threw it into the air as I took a photo, the water freezing instantly in the subzero temperature.

I still have that photo, and it's the strangest thing ever. There's Chris, grinning, pot in hand, King's Peak towering in the background, and in front of him is a long sinuous thing that looks like a giant hotdog with hundreds of spears of ice sticking out everywhere.

This changed the mood for the better, and Chris and I joked around after that, seemingly back to how things used to be. We pulled out cigars and sat puffing on them, even though neither of us were smokers. It was a ritual to celebrate making it as far as we had.

But in retrospect, things hadn't really changed, they'd just lightened up for awhile.

We spent our third day resting, tired and trying to acclimate, half expecting to see Kim's team show up at any time. We didn't understand why they hadn't yet caught up to us.

I realized later that they'd stayed put at basecamp for awhile to organize everything and acclimate. They were from the Alberta prairie and not as used to the altitude as we were, plus it takes longer to get a larger group like that organized and moving.

Instead of Kim's group, what showed up was the wind. A major storm appeared to be coming in, and we knew this could shut us down for some time. These things were virtually impossible to predict, for they rose quickly and unexpectedly from the other side of the mountains in the Gulf of Alaska and swept across to the east, catching up more wind and snow on the way, growing in intensity.

We dragged everything back into the vestibule, again using the sled as a sort of door, cramming its tail into the snow. It actually worked pretty effectively, although some snow still blew in. We were happy for the zipped door between us and the vestibule as the wind shook the tent, howling and moaning. The snow wall we'd built around the tent helped keep it from getting buried.

It was around midnight when we heard voices. I at first thought it was my imagination, then I thought it was a plane.

"Chris, listen," I said. "Hear the plane? Do you think it's come in to rescue someone?"

Chris replied, "Don't be silly. It's the wind. A plane could never land in these conditions."

I listened—it was indeed the wind, but I swore I could hear voices. Finally, there was no denying it, someone was shouting over the wind. It appeared that Kim's group had finally caught up with us.

We were both happy for the company, leaving our tent and warm sleeping bags to help them set up their tents and get settled in. They'd been caught in the blizzard and would've been lost if they hadn't been able to find their way with a map and GPS. They were very happy to see us.

It was a long night, and the next day was even longer, as the wind, instead of letting up, seemed to blow harder. I was afraid to leave the tent, as I thought it would blow away without my weight holding it down. Chris felt the same way, so we took turns going out, though we tried not to go out at all.

We didn't see much of the other group, as everyone was hunkered down. I was glad for all the extra food, for this was exactly the kind of thing I knew could happen from all the stories I'd read about climbing Mount Logan. The northern peaks were always like this, with erratic and unpredictable storms brewing.

Mindful of keeping my pack as light as possible, I'd brought one single book for such an occasion, as had Chris. Mine was John McPhee's "Annals of the Former World," a long tome on the geology of the U.S., and Chris had brought Mark Twain's "Roughing It." We'd picked the books based on length, wanting something that would last for many hours if we found ourselves in a situation like the one we were currently in.

We read and read, switching sides, stretching out, making tea, curling up, and after we'd each finished our book, we traded and kept reading. After the second day of the storm, now our fifth day on the mountain, we started reading passages aloud to each other and commenting on them as if we were in an English Lit. class.

Finally, bored, I got out my notebook and started sketching pictures of pizza, steaks, and whatever delicious food I could think of. We'd only barely started, and I was already craving comfort foods. I'd heard of climbers losing a pound or more a day on high-altitude climbs like this, and it felt like I'd already lost weight, even just resting in the tent.

The next morning we again heard voices, and the unnatural quiet told us the storm had passed through. Kim's group was up and around, and we got up excitedly, packing up our gear, readying to continue.

The other group had set up a cook tent, and it had been blown several hundred yards down the trench. They ran down and retrieved it, and I remarked to Chris that I felt they were being extremely careless to not rope up, as the whole area was a crevasse field. In retrospect, their carelessness was a red flag, but I ignored it.

The skies were still stormy looking, the tail end of the storm passing through. The few extra days had helped us acclimate, and

Chris and I both felt good. Our differences now seemed minor. Everything negative seemed to have dissipated with the storm.

I was soon again wrestling with the toboggan, even though it was now a few pounds lighter from our stay in the tent. No matter what I did, it was impossible to keep its lines from catching in my ski poles, which was very frustrating. I thought about abandoning it, but I decided that carrying all that weight on my back would soon get more tiresome than wrestling with the poles.

I finally stopped and redistributed the weight on the sled, putting the heavy stuff on the bottom and the lighter stuff on top, which helped some.

The storm had now cleared out, leaving skies filled with ice crystals. It was hard to breathe but was incredibly beautiful, making everything look like a snow globe.

We trudged on, again having outpaced Kim's group, though we could see them as small shapes against the horizon behind us. Because there were only two of us, we were capable of making much better time, but I also suspected we were in better shape, having climbed a lot.

It was a beautiful day, and we finally stopped to make lunch and take a break. I'd stepped off a few feet to take a leak when I saw a trackway cutting at a 90° angle from the trench, going to the side. This puzzled me. Why would someone be going across King's Trench? Were they going to climb one of the lower peaks?

I carefully walked over to look at the tracks, but it was hard to tell much except they seemed exceedingly deep. Whoever it was had neither snowshoes nor skis, and yet they'd still managed to have a stride of nearly three feet between each step. I found this incredible. The trackway stretched as far as the eye could see, disappearing in the cliffs.

I called Chris over to have a look, and he too was puzzled. It just seemed so unlikely, and why only one set of tracks? Why perpendicular to us and not parallel?

I thought of an Argentinian woman, 37-year-old Natalia Martinez, who'd tried to solo the peak and been caught in a huge earthquake, necessitating a rescue, but it was rare to solo Logan. Besides, one didn't solo Logan by climbing the wrong direction. It was just too weird.

It was then that Kim's team finally caught up with us. Either we'd slowed down or they were getting their stride, maybe both. I was actually happy for this, as it would make things safer to have more people roped together when we crossed crevasse fields. It was always easier to rescue someone with more people, especially when it came to dragging someone out of a crevasse. I didn't know it, but my thoughts would soon become prophetic.

I thought about the nature of being rescued on Logan as opposed to Denali. Even though the climb up Logan is similar to Denali in its character, Logan is much more remote and isolated. In contrast, Denali has a park service ranger patrol, endless plane traffic, and hundreds of climbers at camp and en route, and even though this can be frustrating, it makes for a safer climb. Logan had none of this.

When Kim's crew caught up with us, I showed them the tracks. One of the guys laughingly remarked that Yeti had found its way to North America, and they all joked about this for awhile, but I noticed Kim looked pretty serious.

She began asking questions the rest of us hadn't considered—had someone become disoriented and stumbled off trail, maybe in the blizzard? Should we follow the tracks and see if they needed help?

Her group had a satellite phone and decided to call out and tell the park rangers what we'd seen. They took GPS coordinates and relayed those, hoping the next air charter could do a flyover and check it out.

We decided to continue forward, for going off-course could be very dangerous. The tracks stretched far across the trench, considerably out of our way, and who knew how old they were?

We now trudged on together, hoping to get to King's Col Camp at 13,500 feet, King's Peak still looming above us to our right. Eventually, we reached another crevasse field and roped up together, carefully using our ski poles to probe ahead, going slow. We wore our harnesses all the time so we didn't have to fumble while roping up in potentially dangerous places.

It was fairly treacherous, but what made it really scary was that the trench itself had narrowed and we were now also in serious avalanche terrain. There was avalanche exposure up most of the route, but we'd now entered a zone where we had to work our way through the rubble from previous slides, the flanks of high mountains towering ominously above on both sides.

No one spoke, and the sound of our skis slowly swishing along gave the scene an eerie feeling. Avalanche responders and beacons were highly recommended by the park, and Chris and I had ours, but I wondered about Kim's group.

My thoughts then wandered to what I would do if I had to help rescue someone. I had a probe and shovel on my toboggan, and my love-hate relationship with the sled turned to love, at least for awhile.

It typically takes two days to get from the King's Trench Camp to the King's Col Camp, and once the trench widened back out and the avalanche danger lessened, we came to the consensus to make camp and try for King's Col the next day.

We'd gained only 1,000 feet of altitude, but the next day would be relatively easy in comparison, even though we would have more avalanche exposure and another crevasse field to cross.

In spite of being stuck in our tents for several days, we were now making good time. I helped Chris stomp down a base, build a snow wall, and pitch our tent. I did notice with concern that the tip of his nose was turning white, and he dutifully put on his face mask. His thermometer now read minus 15°, cold enough for rapid frostbite.

Kim's crew soon had their cook tent up and invited us to have dinner with them. They'd made a big pot of spicy chili, the exact type of food I try to avoid when climbing, even though it was delicious.

Because food supplies are so critical on a trip like this, I felt it appropriate to contribute something back, so I dug out a frosted spice cake that a friend had made for our trip, which was a big hit. I guess Chris also felt like he needed to contribute something, so he pulled out a flask of Scotch whiskey, which was an even bigger hit, at least with several members of Kim's group. I noticed she didn't partake, nor did I.

I was furious, but said nothing. Alcohol and cold and high altitudes are a recipe for disaster, and Chris knew it as well as anyone, if not better. I knew that anyone who drank Chris's whisky could potentially have their judgment and stamina affected the next day, impacting us all. And drinking alcohol can actually help bring on hypothermia, since alcohol causes the blood vessels to open up, causing the body to cool.

Chris became his typical jovial self when drinking, and he sat next to Kim, telling her all about our expedition on Denali in more detail than she probably cared to hear. To me, it seemed like he was bragging.

I said good night to everyone, even though it was still early, and crawled into the tent. My irritation with Chris now burned, not just because of the alcohol, which I knew would slow him down the next day, but also because he seemed to be arrogant in talking about his climbs—at least, that's what I thought my irritation was from, but maybe it was just part of the earlier ongoing disenchantment I was having with our friendship.

I wrote for a bit in my journal, did a sketch of King's Peak, and finally went to bed.

I was tired, and the altitude was bothering me a little, but nothing serious. I just felt more fatigued than I should have. I didn't even wake up when Chris came in, at least not until he started snoring like a freight train—I'd camped with Chris many times and knew this snoring was the result of alcohol. After I bluntly told him to shut up a few times, he finally turned over and seemed to fall into a deep sleep.

It was as dark as it gets up north on a summer night, so I figured it must have been about two a.m., when Chris started talking in his sleep, waking me. This was new, Chris never talked in his sleep, but I could hear him clear as day, though I couldn't quite make out what he was saying. It seemed as if he'd somehow gotten inside my head and was talking gibberish.

I was probably more angry than I should've been, and I was pretty vehement about telling him to shut up, adding a few choice swear words for emphasis. Chris was now awake, sitting up as something was scraping against the tent.

There was something in the vestibule! My first thought went to something stealing the cache, and I quickly snapped on my headlamp. There was no way I was going to let our food be stolen.

I yelled like a pirate at the top of my lungs, thinking it was probably a bear and I would scare it away. Chris seemed totally confused and befuddled, holding his hand up against the glare of my headlamp.

I unzipped the door that led into the vestibule, shining my light all around, but if anything had been in there, it was gone—as was my sled and Chris's pack.

I slipped on my heavy parka and boots and stepped outside, shining my light everywhere, frantic. The sled held almost all our food, and without it, we'd have to borrow Kim's sat phone and call for an early pickup.

I flashed my light all around until I finally saw the sled a good 20 feet from the tent. I ran to it, barely grabbing it—a few moments more and it would've been gone, as it was sliding down the hill, slowly gaining speed. I dragged it back to the tent and secured it in the vestibule, crawling back inside, noting that Chris had grabbed his pack and pulled it inside the tent.

Chris asked what had happened, but I had no answers. He then said that the sled had probably been pushed out of the vestibule by the wind, maybe dragging the pack along with it.

I was once again angry, for Chris apparently hadn't secured the sled properly when he'd come into the tent after I'd gone to sleep. He'd probably been tipsy, and if I hadn't heard him talking in his sleep, the sled would've been long gone, as would've been our chances at climbing Logan. This was exactly the kind of carelessness I'd been worried about earlier. It took me a long time to get back to sleep.

We continued on the next day, neither of us mentioning the incident of the previous night, but Chris seemed quieter than usual.

Kim's group had again camped with us, but as usual, we were far ahead by the time they got up and around.

From now on, as the scenery around us became more and more stunning, the climbs between camps became more and more arduous. We would undoubtedly reach King's Col Camp by evening, but the upcoming stretch was really hairy, replete with both avalanche and crevasse danger almost the entire way.

We debated whether or not to wait for Kim's group so we could all rope up together, but then decided we were getting behind schedule and should just keep going. They didn't have the experience we did, but they knew enough about crevasses by that time to know what to do and what not to do. We hadn't signed on to guide anyone, and we were both getting anxious to make the summit.

But it was only a matter of a half hour or less when we could hear shouts coming from below. I always carry a small monocular, and as I glassed down the slope towards our last camp I could see Kim's group, and one of them was waving what looked to be a red parka.

My heart sank, for I could see two others of the group down on their stomachs looking into what appeared to be a long black line in the snow—a crevasse. I counted the people, and sure enough, there were only four. It appeared someone had fallen in.

We'd just roped through the crevasse field ourselves, and the thought of going back through it again wasn't pleasant. But I felt we had no choice—we had to go back. Both Chris and I had extensive experience in crevasse rescues, and I was sure they would need our help.

Chris wanted to leave our packs and the sled where we'd stopped so we could make better time down, but I insisted we take them with us. Who knew if we would be back up there, and our lives would depend on having our gear.

I was surprised at how quickly we made it back down, following our tracks, which was encouraging. I'd heard that one could ski from the summit to the base camp in a day if they were good skiers, and this confirmed that it might be possible.

I was shocked at what we found. Just like when they'd gone for the cook tent, no one had bothered to rope up, even though they knew they were traversing a crevasse field.

I'd seen that first incident as a red flag, and I now knew I was right. Their group didn't belong on the mountain, they were being so careless. The very fact that they would partake in Chris's alcohol had confirmed that, but this made it even clearer.

Someone was down in the crevasse with no rope, which was going to make a rescue extremely difficult. I wasn't exactly sure who it was, except I knew it wasn't Kim, for she seemed to be the only one calm enough to be trying to organize a rescue. I just hoped we wouldn't be recovering a body at that point.

Chris and I assessed the situation, then decided one of us would go down on a rope to see if the person, a guy named Kurt, was even still alive, and then decide what to do from there.

I thought again of Chris drinking the previous night and decided I would have to be the one to go. Frankly, I didn't trust him to get the job done, knowing that he wasn't at his best.

We soon had a rope set, and I went over the edge. Kurt was only about 25 feet down and had luckily managed to catch his pack on a wedge of ice, which was all that was holding him in place. I knew I had to quickly get a rope around him before the pack straps gave out. They were also cutting into his chest and making it difficult for him to breathe.

Because he wasn't down all that far and was basically unhurt, it was a relatively straightforward rescue. He was wearing his harness, which made things easier, and I soon had him roped up. The group above hoisted him up, and I then jumared my way up, and that was that.

We all stood around for a moment, saying nothing, then everyone silently roped up and we returned to trudging upwards, arriving at the 13,500-foot King's Col Camp later that afternoon.

Everyone was really quiet that night and went to bed early. I think they knew what I was thinking, that they had no business being up there and should go back. But there was no way I was going to tell them that—first of all, they weren't my responsibility, and secondly, I felt that Chris had contributed to their carelessness by providing them with alcohol the previous evening.

I again had trouble sleeping, probably from the altitude. As I tossed and turned, I wondered what had really happened to the sled the previous night. Even if Chris hadn't pulled it into the vestibule, there was no way it would take off down the hill like that on its own, because our snow wall would've stopped it.

We always built a small snow barrier around the tent to keep snow from partly burying us during the night if a wind came up, and the sled would have had to be dragged over that before it could go anywhere. On top of that, Chris's pack was just too heavy for the sled to be able to move it out of the vestibule unless a hurricane-force wind had been blowing.

Thinking that something or someone had tried to take our sled, along with hearing what I'd assumed was Chris's voice at about the same time, well, it all left me feeling very spooked.

On top of all that, while we'd been trudging up the hill to King's Col, I'd caught a glimpse of something in the rocks above us. It was large and covered head to toe in long black hair that blew in the wind, hair way too long to be a bear. It must've seen me looking at it, for it quickly ducked down, but even in that short time, it gave me the creeps.

I'd looked to see if Chris had spotted it also, but he had his head down, looking for crevasses, as he was leading. It all seemed to fit together with something stealing caches, but it also seemed other-worldly, a feeling that was beginning to permeate the entire place.

For some reason, the thought came from nowhere—what if Chris and I had been climbing apart instead of together when the figure in the rocks appeared above us? What exactly was it? I thought it might be prudent for us to stay with Kim's group from there on out.

Each camp we reached was more rewarding than the last, but the altitude was having an effect on both Chris and I. Actually, we both knew we should be acclimating better than we were, as we were both now getting headaches and having shortness of breath, as well as losing our appetites, and we weren't even all that high yet.

That night, after a big dinner that neither of us really wanted and lots of hot tea, I decided to see what Chris was thinking. He'd been uncharacteristically quiet all day. We were both in our sleeping bags, hunkering down for the night.

"Chris," I said measuredly. "Last night, I heard what I thought was you talking in your sleep, but it was odd, almost like it was in my head, and you never talk in your sleep plus it was gibberish, like a monkey. Shortly after that, I heard something brush against the side of the tent, and when I looked outside, the sled was gone. In addition, your heavy pack was out of the vestibule."

I paused, then added, "How would you explain all that? Tell me how my sled, which I barely caught from running away down the mountain, and your heavy pack could both be outside our foot-tall snow wall."

Chris shook his head in chagrin. "I told you, it was the wind. It came up under the vestibule and blew everything out. We need to get a tent with a vestibule floor. A really heavy wind could blow stuff over the wall, it wasn't that tall."

"But there was no wind," I replied, frustrated.

"It was blowing when you were asleep. It woke me up," Chris replied. "You obviously slept through it. It pushed everything out of the vestibule and over the wall, and then it took the sled awhile before it started taking off, and you caught it just in time."

"Okay, I'll grant you that, but how do you explain the figure I saw up in the rocks? When it saw me looking at it, it ducked down. It was coal black. It wasn't my imagination, Chris."

Chris answered, "Buckaroo, remember how we've talked about this thing called mountain madness? Remember the guy who reported seeing heavy road equipment near the top of Aconcagua? You've heard the stories just like I have. And that's what I think you saw on that cliff—a big something that wasn't real. Mountain madness had you in its grip for a moment."

"Give me a break," I replied with anger. "If anyone was a bit off their rocker, it was you from too much whiskey the night before."

"OK, I know that irritated you, and I'm sorry. I shouldn't have brought it with me."

"It's bad for hypothermia, you know that," I replied, but since Chris seemed sincerely contrite, I let it go.

Chris and I had talked about mountain madness a lot before, as it fascinated us. We'd both seen it in other climbers, as well as maybe having touches of it ourselves. It was just beginning to be recognized as a real ailment by the medical community, something separate from all the other things that can go wrong when you climb, though mountaineers had known about it for decades.

Anyone who's climbed big peaks for long has heard of "third man syndrome," a presence that provides help when things are going wrong, often by guiding a lost climber back to their camp. But there were also plenty of times when the opposite occurred, when a climber thought he was hearing voices giving him good advice that had actually turned out to be potentially fatal.

The affliction was primarily characterized by hallucinations, with the sufferer seeming perfectly normal in all other ways. Unlike physical ailments like pulmonary and cerebral edema, mountain madness wasn't fatal, though researchers thought it might be the source of a number of inexplicable accidents and misjudgments. They were beginning to think it was a form of temporary high-altitude psychosis.

I crawled down into my sleeping bag, muttering something to the effect that, "I know what I saw, Chris, and it was real," but wondering if he might be right. It didn't make sense to see something black way up in the rocks on an unnamed ridge that had probably never been climbed.

But as I drifted off, I could once again see the mysterious trackway, and I was pretty sure I was sane, at least as sane as any climber could be. I did vow, however, to be especially careful, just in case. I would defer any important decisions to Chris, or better yet, to Kim, if she were around.

The next day would be our eighth day on the mountain, and we hoped to make the next camp by dark, even though it was normally a two-day effort. We knew we were getting closer to the top with every step, and at this point we both just wanted to summit and go home.

Even Chris was complaining about not feeling well, and I hoped he wasn't coming down with something serious. I was actually feeling a bit better, somewhat stronger, and was now beginning to really enjoy the views. Once we got to Camp 3, which sat at 15,700 feet, the summit was within our reach, just a couple of days away.

We would continue to climb with Kim's group, even though they sometimes held us to a slower pace than we preferred. Every time I thought about telling Chris we should break away and go faster, I recalled the black figure in the rocks and said nothing.

The whole time, we watched the sky for changes in the weather, for this would be the only thing that could stop us at this point, barring an accident. Any little wisp of cloud was a matter of much deliberation and thought, and our eyes often turned to the west, the direction from which the big storms would come.

The only forms of communication in the St. Elias Range are devices that rely on satellites, so we couldn't call out for weather reports. I knew that Kim's group had an expensive sat phone, but I wasn't sure if they were doing any weather tracking with it or not, but I figured that they would tell us if they did know of something coming in. We were getting more and more anxious to get to the summit and back down.

And the whole time we climbed the trench I looked for signs of climbers ahead of us, but I never saw any, nor did we find any caches. Kim's group had told us the rangers at Haines Junction had said the park was talking about banning caches entirely.

So, that next morning, we got a really early start and it seemed that everyone was feeling stronger. We slogged up the mountain, stopping only for quick breaks, and by midnight, to my amazement, we actually made it to Camp 3.

I think everyone was feeling summit fever, knowing we were only a few days from the top. I was amazed that Kim's group had climbed so strong, and after a quick dinner, we crawled into our tents, exhausted. I noticed that Kim's group didn't even bother to set up their cook tent.

Kim's group had been changed by Kurt's accident in the crevasse, and they now seemed to be taking the climb much more seriously. In fact, Kurt had become a sort of safety patrol, always making sure everyone was buckled up and tied in.

Chris and I always led, having more crevasse experience, but I noticed Kurt was always right behind us, making sure all was well, maybe as a sort of penance for the trouble he'd caused. In any case, they were now climbing more like pros and less like a bunch of happy-go-lucky kids.

I was happy to see this, especially since it meant Chris and I could go off the mountain at our own pace after we'd summited and not worry about them. We were both strong skiers, and I hoped to be able to ski down in one day.

That night, I again woke to Chris talking in his sleep, but instead of waking him, I tried to understand what he was saying. It was garbled, and once again seemed to be bypassing my ears and going straight into my brain. I knew that wasn't possible and was probably a sensation caused by the altitude. But this time, it wasn't gibberish.

"Now that we're close, it's very important that we rest a lot," Chris said. "We won't have a lot of strength, and I think it's best we leave everything at the last camp while we summit."

I didn't answer, for I knew he was sound asleep, but I was once again irritated. He was saying the exact opposite of what we should really do.

If we wanted to summit, we needed to set a pace and stick with it, not take breaks all the time. Every time you stop for a break, your body has to reset when you restart. Unless you're extraordinarily tired, you should just stay at pace and keep going.

But maybe Chris was right about leaving everything at the last camp. It would make things much easier, and I wouldn't be pulling that damn sled to the summit.

I'd read that it typically takes about 15 hours from the Summit Plateau Camp to the summit and back again, so there really was no need to carry all our gear to the top, as we'd be back at that camp that same day. The odds of someone stealing our cache at that altitude seemed small.

When I woke early the next dawn, I could see Mt. Logan towering over us. I knew we must look like tiny dark specks against the white snow to anyone on its summit.

It was one of the most spectacular sights of all my mountaineering career. The mountain was completely white, all of its ridges and rock outcroppings completely buried in snow, and as I stood in wonder, alpenglow began to light its summit in subtle shades of pink.

Someone was now standing by me, and I turned to see Kim. We really hadn't talked too much on the entire expedition, primarily because I was usually holed up in my tent, mad at Chris over something or other.

She wrapped her arm in mine in what I took as a gesture of friendship, as well as from being cold. It was bitter, but I knew as soon as the sun rose over the mountains it would warm up, the reflective surface of the snow acting like a heat source.

We talked about trying to make it to the Summit Plateau Camp at 17,600 feet in one day, which we both thought was quite possible, even though some people take two.

There was an intermediary camp between here and there, Camp 4, but once one reached that, it was all downhill to the Summit Plateau Camp, which sat on a plateau that rose again to the mountain's top.

"Are you guys strong skiers?" I asked.

"We all ski pretty well. Why do you ask?" she replied.

"I've heard you can ski to the bottom in one day if you're a good skier and follow your tracks. Chris and I are going to try. It would be good for us to all stay together. If we can get to the Summit Plateau Camp today, we could be off the mountain day after tomorrow."

Kim said it was a good plan, one she would mention to her group, as she knew they were getting tired and anxious to get down off the mountain. She knew they wanted to spend a day here to regroup, but she personally wanted to keep going and would try to talk them into it.

The more I talked to her, the better I liked her, but I knew that even if we were to ever have a relationship, my living in the U.S. and her in Canada would probably pose some difficult barriers.

She seemed to like me too, and as she stood there, her arm in mine, watching the alpenglow on the mountain, I felt very close to her.

She then asked, "Are you superstitious?"

I felt it was a strange thing to ask, but I said, "No, generally not. Why?"

She replied, "Before we decided to climb Mt. Logan, I did a lot of research. I came upon several stories about people who had heard and seen strange things. They mostly wrote it off to the altitude, but it gave me pause."

She continued, "But last night, something was messing with my tent—it was almost as if someone was trying to pick it up, and I could hear some of the guy lines snap out of the ice. I thought it was some of the guys playing a prank, but it seemed highly unlikely, as everyone was so tired. Besides, who wants to play pranks at minus 20°? But come look."

We walked over to her tent, where several of the guy lines were indeed pulled from the ice. But what was strange was that there were no tracks anywhere, no sign that anyone had been outside her tent.

"You're not being superstitious, Kim," I replied. "We've been having odd things happen, too—something tried to steal our sled and pack. Chris said it was just the wind, but I also saw something strange."

I then told her about seeing the figure in the rocks. Kim replied with something that left me feeling a grave concern.

"You know our cook tent? There was no way it could've been blown down the mountain like that, as we'd staked it deep into the ice in anticipation of high winds—I think it was tampered with. When we saw it down the mountain, we all kind of freaked out, and that's why we didn't rope up. We'd be warned about leaving caches, so we'd taken our sleds and packs into our tents, but the cook tent had our breakfast in it. When we retrieved it, everything was there except the food."

I was silent, not sure what to say, but we finally agreed we should all stay together from there on out.

Chris and the rest of the group were now stirring, and we joined them, drinking hot tea and eating breakfast. We decided to try for the Summit Plateau Camp today, but if anyone got fatigued, we would stop at Camp 4.

It seemed unreal to everyone that we were so close to the top. If all went well, we would be trying for the summit the next day. So far, the weather seemed to be holding, and everyone said they felt strong and well rested, in spite of the long day yesterday.

When we got to Camp 4, everyone wanted to continue, seeing it was now downhill to the summit plateau, so we kept going, now making good time. Finally, tired and weary, we made it to the Summit Plateau Camp late that evening. We were excited, knowing that if all went well, we'd summit Logan the next day.

Kim's group again set up the cook tent, and we had a huge dinner, partly because we wanted to celebrate, but also because we wanted to build up our reserves as much as we could for the big day tomorrow.

Everyone was happy and talking, and I hoped Chris didn't have any more whiskey in his pack, because I knew he would be likely to pull it out. I found out later that he did but had decided to save it for base camp.

I crawled into our tent and tried to decide whether or not to leave everything at camp or take it with me, thinking of Chris talking in his sleep, telling me to leave everything at the last camp. I felt a shiver go through me, wondering if I had really heard Chris talking or if it were something else.

But I decided I would go ahead and take his advice and leave the tent and sled at the camp, but would load my pack with enough food to get to the summit and back down to base camp. I would also take my sleeping bag, the bivy sack I carried for emergencies, the stove and fuel, and my survival gear, just in case.

It would be a heavy pack, but I would have everything I needed with me. That way, if something happened to the tent and gear at the summit camp, I could still make it back down.

I divvied the food up and put half of it on Chris's sleeping bag. He could make his own decision as to whether to carry it to the top or not. I then crawled into my sleeping bag and tried to sleep. I had a headache and my legs were restless, and the air seemed dreadfully thin. I could hear everyone talking and laughing over by the cook tent, and I wondered why they were so happy, since we still had thousands of feet to go.

But instead of going to sleep, I found myself thinking of my mom and dad far away in the California mountains, probably wondering if I were dead or alive, even though they were used to my shenanigans. I knew they were getting older and probably tired of worrying about me, assuming they even still did. I finally took a sleeping pill as a last resort and was soon out.

I woke around three a.m., noting that Chris had put the extra food in his pack after I'd gone to sleep. I crawled out of the tent and started melting snow on the little stove, Chris still sleeping.

I was soon dressed and ready to go. I still wasn't hungry and had a headache, but I was eager to get going, irritated that the others were asleep. I thought about going alone, but decided I would wait for Chris, restless as I was.

I stomped around for while, trying to get warm, then finally started singing "Taps" at the top of my lungs, then shouting stupid things like, "Rise and shine!"

I felt justified in waking everyone, as it was summit day, and we had a long trek ahead of us. I thought I would feel more excited than I did, but all I really wanted was to get it over with and get back to camp.

Everyone was finally up, irritated with me, but also anxious to summit. One of Kim's group pulled me aside at breakfast to tell me that they'd called out on their sat phone for a weather report and had been told a big front was coming in and was expected to hit within 48 hours, maybe less.

He said his group had decided to go ahead and summit, but he wanted to make sure that Chris and I knew about the storm. If we could summit and get back to camp by dark, we could ski out the next day and hopefully beat the bad weather. Even if we had to hunker down at base camp for a few days, we'd be fine until a plane could come get us.

We were soon on our way again. The movement warmed up both my body and my mind, and I began to feel a sense of exhilaration, our goal was so close. Typically, the day you summit a big peak is usually the hardest, as you're fatigued and at the highest altitude, but this day seemed easier than most.

I knew some of it was mental, as I was happy the trip would soon be over, but it also seemed like a fairly easy climb. The map showed no crevasse danger, as we were now basically above the glacier. For the first time, we didn't rope up, instead walking single file.

Kim and I hadn't talked much since the previous morning, mostly because I was either off by myself or in my tent. I suspected the others were beginning to think I was a bit sullen, but I didn't care. After all, I hadn't signed up to go on their expedition, it was supposed to be just me and Chris. If our original plans had held, we probably would've been off the mountain a couple of days ago.

On we went, and soon tendrils of clouds flew high above and small gusts of wind came in, reminding us to hurry. Chris and Kim and I were now climbing together, the other four somewhat behind us, as the three of us had a faster pace.

Chris and Kim were behind me as I broke trail, and once again I could hear Chris talking about himself, bragging. I shook my head in disgust and upped my pace until I was well ahead of them and finally out of sight.

It was then that I realized how black my feelings towards Chris had become. He was talking to a woman I'd met in a bar, someone I barely even knew and who was maybe married, yet I was jealous. It was ridiculous. I needed to back off and get my head together.

I suddenly felt fatigued, and I knew it was partly mental. I recalled drifting off to sleep in Haines Junction, deciding not to climb

Logan. I was beginning to wish I'd listened to myself. I would be home right now, sitting in my big recliner, maybe even watching something like the Andy Griffith Show, which for some reason sounded really nice. I shook my head at the irony, as I never watched anything, preferring to read instead.

Before I knew it, I was on the summit of Mount Logan, standing at 19,551 feet. The view literally took my breath away, and a wind rose from far below, swirling snow around my feet, portent of the coming storm.

I was the first of our group to summit, not that it meant anything to me, other than I could sit and rest for a bit while waiting for the others to catch up. I pulled a small tin holding hard candies from my pocket and fumbled with it, the wind trying to take it from my hands, then sat back on my heels and waited for the others.

The winds were picking up by the moment, and I wished everyone would hurry up and get there so we could turn around and go back. The view was incredible, but it seemed lost on me, as I just wanted to go down.

In the meantime, I'd almost forgotten that I'd promised to leave something for a friend, a small Tibetan prayer flag. My good friend Joan had recently lost her husband to an avalanche in Alaska's Chugach Mountains, and she'd asked me to place the flag on Mt. Logan in his memory. She felt that his spirit would be with us on our climb.

I carefully unwrapped the flag from my pocket, then dug a hole with my ice axe in the snow under a nearby rock, stuffing the small flag in so it wouldn't blow away. That probably wasn't what Joan had pictured, but it was the best I could do.

That done, I could now see two figures coming through the swirling snow. It had to be Chris and Kim. I stood, my heavy pack still on my back, waiting for them to reach the summit.

As they slowly approached, it was then that I saw the spider. It was unbelievable, but there was a black spider resting on top of the snow, and how the wind kept from blowing it away was beyond me. I bent down to look closer at it. It was alive!

I took the small tin from my pocket, scooped up the spider, and carefully closed the lid, using my body to block the wind. I would take it back to my buddy the entomologist. Maybe he would have some idea how a spider got to the top of a 19,500 foot mountain surrounded by ice fields and lived to tell about it.

For a moment, I felt bad, knowing that the spider was sure to die in the tin, feeling that I had tampered with nature. I wondered if the spider would be like a climber sitting in an ice cave in a whiteout, wondering if it would survive, knowing the odds were against it. But I also knew its chances of surviving on the mountain were zero.

I sat on my haunches, eyes closed. The wind was now starting to howl, and I knew my thinking was getting clouded. In fact, I'd forgotten all about Chris and Kim heading up the summit. I looked up to see them both standing in front of me, looking down on me, backlit by the sun shining through a thin mist.

It took awhile, but I eventually realized it wasn't Chris and Kim. There were indeed others on the mountain. They had summited behind me, and I wondered why they'd chosen to wear black parkas and pants covered with long flowing hair, just like the figure I'd seen in the rocks, and why they seemed to loom over me, so much bigger.

Somehow, my mind drifted into thinking that black would be a good choice for climbers, as it would soak up the heat. Maybe when I got back I would suggest it to some gear company and they would give me some kind of bonus for my clever discovery.

Now the figures were talking to me, but I couldn't see their mouths move through the swirling snow, it felt like the sound was in my head, just like when Chris had been talking in his sleep.

"We know how tired you must be. Let us carry your pack down for you."

I was moved by their concern, but I'd stubbornly hauled all that gear up the mountain, and there was no way I would part with it.

"No, I'm fine," I replied.

It felt like my words were being blown out to the Gulf of Alaska, and I wondered why I could barely hear myself through the wind, yet I could understand them so clearly.

Now the other was speaking, his eyes glowing red even in the bright sunlight. I wondered if he weren't going snow blind and why he wasn't wearing goggles.

"It's really a long ways up this mountain," he said. "But we know of a quicker way down. If you go over to the edge with me you can see down forever. There's deep snow down there, and it's very soft. If you jump, you'll save yourself having to trudge down thousands of feet. Others have done it, and your friends can come and pick you up down there. Leave your pack here—you won't need it, and you'll go faster without it."

It suddenly sounded like the perfect thing to do. I could get down quickly and soon be home, sitting in my recliner, headache gone, drinking hot tea.

I started for the edge, the two figures following behind, one lightly pulling on my pack as if he wanted to carry it for me. Now that I was standing near them, I marveled at how huge they were.

Then, for some reason, Chris's words came back to me: "We've all heard the stories, Buckaroo, it's mountain madness. It had you in its grip for a moment."

Of course! The figures weren't real—I was hallucinating! If I listened to them, I would soon fall to my death!

I turned quickly, laughing madly, pushing them aside and literally running to the summit, just in time to see Chris and Kim walk up. I looked back—the two figures had disappeared.

Mountain madness indeed, and I blanched at how close I'd come to falling prey to my own dementia. Chris had been right. His words had saved my life.

I sensed something was wrong from the expression on their faces, then Kim said, "We have to go back. Kurt's getting pulmonary edema, and the others are trying to get him down quickly. I'm glad they're doctors and know what to do. He was somewhat in shock from the crevasse rescue—we shouldn't have let him continue, and now he's in a bad way. We need to follow them and be there when the plane arrives, especially with this storm coming in. They're trying to get out today."

Pulmonary edema is one of the most common killers on the big peaks, filling your lungs with fluid, and yet it has a simple cure: get the victim down to lower altitude quickly. Often, by the time the victim reaches a lower altitude, they've completely recovered.

We quickly hiked back down to the Summit Plateau Camp and collected our tents and put on our skis as fast as we could. Kim's group was long gone, trying to get Kurt down quickly. We didn't catch up with them until almost at basecamp, where they told us that Kurt had recovered enough after a few thousand feet that they were all able to make good time. They'd called on the sat phone, and it wouldn't be long until the plane would come to take us away, though it could haul only two at a time.

I told everyone about my hallucination. I knew it had been a close call, and I thanked Chris for reminding me that one's senses don't always see reality. He said nothing.

It took the plane several trips to get us all out, and Chris and I were the last to go. Once back at the hanger along Kluane Lake, we looked incredibly haggard and tired.

Everyone else had already been shuttled back to Haines Junction by the time we got there—except Kim, who had dutifully waited for us.

It was late by the time we got back to town, and as the shuttle dropped Kim off at the cabin they'd all rented, we said our goodbyes.

I had mixed feelings, hating to see Kim pass from my life, yet happy to be off the mountain. Though we'd exchanged numbers, I knew the logistics were such that we'd probably never see each other again—and it did indeed turn out to be the last time I was in Canada.

But I'll never forget the last thing Kim told me before getting off the shuttle. She looked at me and said, "Those figures you hallucinated up there? They were real. Chris and I saw them too."

With that, she was gone, leaving my heart colder than it had been at the summit of that immense massif itself.

It's not far from Haines Junction to Whitehorse, and the next day, Chris dropped me off at the airport there. I gave him enough gas money to get home, which I didn't mind, as that had been part of the original deal.

He didn't seem to care that I was bailing on him, and there wasn't much he could say anyway, especially when I told him that I was still suffering from mountain madness.

He knew I was being sarcastic, as what I'd seen had really existed, yet I realized that he'd inadvertently saved my life, and I was appreciative. If I'd known the figures at the top of Mt. Logan were real, I think they could've persuaded me to jump, given my fatigue.

As I sat waiting at the Whitehorse airport, I remembered the small tin and took it from my pocket to see if the spider had survived. Amazingly, it had, so I went outside and set it free in some nearby bushes. I didn't have the heart to see it die.

Its ordeal was over, just as was mine. We would both hopefully end up someplace better than where we'd been.

I was soon back home in Missoula, where I was ready to settle down and re-plot my future, which I knew wouldn't have any climbing expeditions in it.

Like I'd figured, I never saw Kim again, though Chris did. I knew he would take his time getting back, as he had no choice, driving that slow bus, but I didn't think he would end up spending three months in Edmonton.

He'd followed Kim home like a little puppy, and though they became friends, that was the extent of it, as I think she'd seen enough on the mountain to know that she didn't want to get involved with him.

He eventually came back to Montana, but only after he'd had to sell the old bus for travel money, which neither of us considered much of a loss. He'd hitched a ride back with some young dirtbag climbers, who I'm sure he regaled all the way with his wild stories. I've often wondered if he told the one about mountain madness on Mt. Logan.

Chris still sleeps on my porch occasionally, which I don't mind, though I do worry about him more since his hair is now showing some gray and he seems to be getting more and more arthritic, which

I'm sure his drinking doesn't help. We're still friends, though not as close, and I find I have more patience for his shenanigans than I once did, yet I feel more detached from him. I'm selling my house and going back to the Sierras, and I hope he does OK without me.

He's stopped climbing, which he says is because he's too stiff. I know this is true, but there's more—he says he's worried about mountain madness and that something bad might happen to him.

I just let it go. He knows the truth as well as I do—he knows I didn't have mountain madness—but he just doesn't want to admit there's something out there he can't explain. It's just too scary.

ABOUT THE AUTHOR

Rusty Wilson is a fly-fishing guide based in Colorado and Montana. He's well-known for his dutch-oven cookouts and campfires, where he's heard some pretty wild stories about the creatures in the woods, especially Bigfoot.

Whether you're a Bigfoot believer or not, we hope you enjoyed this book, and we know you'll enjoy Rusty's many others, the first of which is *Rusty Wilson's Bigfoot Campfire Stories*, as well as his popular *Chasing After Bigfoot: My Search for North America's Most Elusive Creature*.

Rusty's books come in ebook format, as well as in print and audio.

You'll also enjoy the first book in the Bud Shumway mystery series, a Bigfoot mystery, *The Ghost Rock Cafe*.

Other offerings from Yellow Cat Publishing include an RV series by RV expert Sunny Skye, which includes *Living the Simple RV Life*. And don't forget to check out the books by Sunny's friend, Bob Davidson: On the Road with Joe and Any Road, USA.